THE MONKEY
GRAMMARIAN

TITLES BY OCTAVIO PAZ AVAILABLE FROM
ARCADE PUBLISHING

Alternating Current
Conjunctions and Disjunctions
Marcel Duchamp: Appearance Stripped Bare
The Monkey Grammarian
On Poets and Others

THE MONKEY
GRAMMARIAN

OCTAVIO PAZ

TRANSLATED FROM THE SPANISH BY
HELEN LANE

ARCADE PUBLISHING · NEW YORK

FIRST ARCADE EDITION 1990

Originally published in Spain in Editorial Seix Barral, S.A., under the title *El Mono Gramático*

Library of Congress Cataloging-in-Publication Data
  Paz, Octavio, 1914–
    [Mono gramático. English]
    The monkey grammarian / Octavio Paz ; translated from the Spanish by Helen Lane. —1st Arcade ed.
      p. cm.
    Translation of : El mono gramático.
    ISBN 1-55970-135-8
    I. Title
  PQ7297.P285M613 1990
  864—dc20   90-24582

Published in the United States by Arcade Publishing, Inc., New York, by arrangement with Seaver Books
Distributed by Time Warner Book Group

Visit our Web site at www.arcadepub.com

10 9 8 7 6 5 4 3 2

Designed by Beth Tondreau

CCP

PUBLISHED IN THE UNITED STATES OF AMERICA

HANUMĀN, HANUMAT, HANŪMAT. A celebrated monkey chief. He was able to fly and is a conspicuous figure in the *Rāmāyana*. . . . Hanumān leaped from India to Ceylon in one bound; tore up trees, carried away the Himalayas, seized the clouds and performed many other wonderful exploits. . . . Among his other accomplishments, Hanumān was a grammarian; and the *Rāmāyana* says: "The chief of monkeys is perfect; no one equals him in the sāstras, in learning, and in ascertaining the sense of the scriptures (or in moving at will). It is well known that Hanumān was the ninth author of grammar."

John Dowson, M. R. A. S.,
A Classical Dictionary of Hindu Mythology

TO MARIE JOSÉ

THE MONKEY
GRAMMARIAN

The best thing to do will be to choose the path to Galta, traverse it again (invent it as I traverse it), and without realizing it, almost imperceptibly, go to the end—without being concerned about what "going to the end" means or what I meant when I wrote that phrase. At the very beginning of the journey, already far off the main highway, as I walked along the path that leads to Galta, past the little grove of banyan trees and the pools of foul stagnant water, through the Gateway fallen into ruins and into the main courtyard bordered by dilapidated houses, I also had no idea where I was going, and was not concerned about it. I wasn't asking myself questions: I was walking, merely walking, with no fixed itinerary in mind. I was simply setting forth to meet . . . what? I didn't know at the time, and I still don't know. Perhaps that is why I wrote "going to the end": in order to find out, in order to discover what there is after the end. A verbal trap; after the end there is nothing, since if there were something, the end would not be the end. Nonetheless, we are always setting forth to meet . . . , even though we know that there is nothing, or no one, awaiting us. We go along, without a fixed itinerary, yet at the same time with an end (what end?) in mind, and with the aim of reaching the end. A search for the end, a dread of the end: the obverse and the reverse of the same act. Without this end that constantly eludes us we would not journey forth, nor would there be any paths. But the end is the refutation and the condemnation of the path: at the end the path dissolves, the meeting fades away to nothingness. And the end—it too fades away to nothingness.

Setting forth once more, embarking upon the search once again: the narrow path that snakes among livid rocks and desolate, camel-colored hills; white houses hanging suspended from cliffs, looking as though they were about to let go and fall on the wayfarer's head; the smell of sweating hides and cow dung; the buzz of afternoon; the screams of monkeys leaping about amid the branches of the trees or scampering along the flat rooftops or swinging from the railings of a balcony; overhead, birds circling and the bluish spirals of smoke rising from kitchen fires; the almost pink light on the stones; the taste of salt on parched lips; the sound of loose earth slithering away beneath one's feet; the dust that clings to one's sweat-drenched skin, makes one's eyes red, and

Hanumān, drawing on paper, Rajasthan, 18th century. Collection of Marie José Paz (photograph by Daniel David).

chokes one's lungs; images, memories, fragmentary shapes and forms—all those sensations, visions, half-thoughts that appear and disappear in the wink of an eye, as one sets forth to meet. . . . The path also disappears as I think of it, as I say it.

Through my window, some three hundred yards away, the dark green bulk of the grove of trees, a mountain of leaves and branches that sways back and forth and threatens to fall over. A populace of beeches, birches, aspens, and ash trees gathered together on a slight prominence, their tops all capsizing, transformed into a single liquid mass, the crest of a heaving sea. The wind shakes them and lashes them until they howl in agony. The trees twist, bend, straighten up again with a deafening creak and strain upward as though struggling to uproot themselves and flee. No, they do not give in. The pain of roots and broken limbs, the fierce stubbornness of plants, no less powerful than that of animals and men. If these trees were suddenly to start walking, they would destroy everything in their path. But they choose to remain where they are: they do not have blood or nerves, only sap, and instead of rage or fear, a silent tenacity possesses them. Animals flee or attack; trees stay firmly planted where they are. Patience: the heroism of plants. Being neither a lion nor a serpent: being a holm-oak, a piru-tree.

Clouds the color of steel have filled the sky; it is almost white in the distance, gradually turning darker and darker toward the center, just above the grove of trees, where it gathers in violent, deep purple masses. The trees shriek continuously beneath these malevolent accumulations. Toward the right the grove is a little less dense and the leafy intertwining branches of two beeches form a dark archway. Beneath the arch there is a bright, extraordinarily quiet space, a sort of pool of light that is not completely visible from here, since the horizontal line of the neighbors' wall cuts across it. It is a low wall, a brick surface laid out in squares like graph paper, over which there extends the cold green stain of a rosebush. In certain spots where there are no leaves, the knotty trunk and the bifurcations of its spreading branches, bristling with thorns, can be seen. A profusion of arms, pincers, claws and other extremities studded with spiny barbs: I had never thought of a rosebush as an immense crab. The patio must be some forty yards square; it is paved in cement, and along with the rose-bush, a minuscule meadow dotted with daisies sets it off. In one corner there is a small table of dark wood which has long since fallen apart. What could it have been used for? Perhaps it was once a plant stand. Every day, for

Five-headed Hanumān, painting, Jammu, 18th century.

several hours, as I read or write, it is there in front of me, but even though I am quite accustomed to its presence, it continues to seem incongruous to me: what is it doing there? At times I am aware of it as one would be aware of an error, or an untoward act; at other times I see it as a critique. A critique of the rhetoric of the trees and the wind. In the opposite corner is the garbage can, a metal container three feet high and a foot and a half in diameter: four wire feet that support a cylinder with a rusty cover, lined with a plastic sack to hold the refuse. The sack is a fiery red color. Crabs again. The table and the garbage can, the brick walls and the cement paving enclose space. Do they enclose it or are they doors that open onto it?

Beneath the arch of the beeches the light has deepened, and its fixity, hemmed in by the heaving shadows of the foliage, is very nearly absolute. As I gaze at it, I too remain completely at rest. Or better put: my thought draws back in upon itself and remains perfectly still for a long moment. Is this repose the force that prevents the trees from fleeing and the sky from falling apart? Is it the *gravity* of this moment? Yes, I am well aware that nature—or what we call nature: that totality of objects and processes that surrounds us and that alternately creates us and devours us—is neither our accomplice nor our confidant. It is not proper to project our feelings onto things or to attribute our own sensations and passions to them. Can it also be improper to see in them a guide, a way of life? To learn the art of remaining motionless amid the agitation of the whirlwind, to learn to remain still and to be as transparent as this fixed light amid the frantic branches—this may be a program for life. But the bright spot is no longer an oval pool but an incandescent triangle, traversed by very fine flutings of shadow. The triangle stirs almost imperceptibly, until little by little a luminous boiling takes place, at the outer edges first, and then, with increasing fury, in its fiery center, as if all this liquid light were a seething substance gradually becoming yellower and yellower. Will it explode? The bubbles continually flare up and die away, in a rhythm resembling that of panting breath. As the sky grows darker, the bright patch of light dims and begins to flicker; it might almost be a lamp about to go out amid turbulent shadows. The trees remain exactly where they were, although they are now clad in another light.

Fixity is always momentary. It is an equilibrium, at once precarious and perfect, that lasts the space of an instant: a flickering of the light, the appearance of a cloud, or a slight change in temperature is enough to break the repose-pact and unleash the series of metamorphoses. Each metamorphosis, in turn, is another moment of fixity succeeded by another change and another unexpected equilibrium. No one is alone, and each change here brings about another change there. No one is alone and nothing is solid: change is comprised of fixities that are momentary accords. Ought I to say that the form of change is fixity, or more precisely, that change is an endless search for fixity? A nostalgia for inertia: indolence and its frozen paradises. Wisdom lies neither in fixity nor in change, but in the dialectic between the two. A constant coming and going: wisdom lies in the momentary. It is transition. But the moment I say *transition*, the spell is broken. Transition is not wisdom, but a simple going toward. . . . Transition vanishes: only thus is it transition.

 I did not want to think again about Galta and the dusty road that leads to it, and yet they are coming back now. They return furtively, despite the fact that I do not see them, I feel that they are here again, and are waiting to be named. No thought occurs to me, I am not thinking about anything, my mind is a real "blank": like the word *transition* when I say it, like the path as I walk along it, everything vanishes as I think of Galta. As I think of it? No, Galta is here, it has slithered into a corner of my thoughts and is lurking there with that indecisive existence (which nonetheless is demanding, precisely on account of its indecision) of thoughts not completely thought through, not wholly expressed. The imminence of presence before it presents itself. But there is no such presence—only an expectation comprised of irritation and impotence. Galta is not here: it is awaiting me at the end of this phrase. It is awaiting me in order to disappear. In the face of the emptiness that its name conjures up I feel the same perplexity as

when confronted with its hilltops leveled off by centuries of wind and its yellowish plains on which, during the long months of drouth, when the heat pulverizes the rocks and the sky looks as though it will crack like the earth, the dust clouds rise. Reddish, grayish, or dusky apparitions that suddenly come gushing forth like a waterspout or a geyser, except that dust whirlwinds are images of thirst, malevolent celebrations of aridity. Phantoms that dance like whirling dervishes, that advance, retreat, fall motionless, disappear here, reappear there: apparitions without substance, ceremonies of dust and air. What I am writing is also a ceremony, the whirling of a word that appears and disappears as it circles round and round. I am erecting towers of air.

But it is on the other side of the mountain range that dust storms are frequent, on the great plain, not amid these slopes and ravines. Here the terrain is much rougher and more broken than on the other side, although it availed Galta nothing to take shelter beneath the skirts of the mountain range. On the contrary, its situation exposed it even more to the inroads of the desert. All these undulating surfaces, winding ravines, and gorges are the channels and beds of streams that no longer exist today. These sandy mounds were once covered with trees. The traveler makes his way among dilapidated dwellings: the landscape too has crumbled and fallen to ruins. I read a description dating from

1891: "The way the sandy desert is encroaching on the town should be noticed. It has caused one large suburb to be deserted and the houses and gardens are going to ruin. The sand has even drifted up the ravines of the hills. This evil ought to be arrested at any cost by planting." Less than twenty years later, Galta was abandoned. Not for long however: first monkeys and then bands of wandering pariahs occupied the ruins.

It is not more than an hour's walk away. One leaves the highway on one's left, winds one's way amid rocky hills and climbs upward along ravines that are equally arid. A desolation that is not so much grim as touchingly sad. A landscape of bones. The remains of temples and dwellings, archways that lead to courtyards choked with sand, façades behind which there is nothing save piles of rubble and garbage, stairways that lead to nothing but emptiness, terraces that have fallen in, pools that have become giant piles of excrement. After making one's way across this rolling terrain, one descends to a broad, bare plain. The path is strewn with sharp rocks and one soon tires. Despite the fact that it is now four o'clock in the afternoon, the ground is still burning hot. Sparse little bushes, thorny plants, vegetation that is twisted and stunted. Up ahead, not far in the distance, the starving mountain. A skin of stones, a mountain covered with scabs. There is a fine dust in the air, an impalpable substance that irritates and makes one feel queasy. Things seem stiller beneath this light that is weightless and yet oppressive. Perhaps the word is not *stillness* but *persistence*: things persist beneath the humiliation of the light. And the light persists. Things are more thinglike, everything is persisting in being, merely being. One crosses the stony bed of a little dry stream and the sound of one's footsteps on the stones is reminiscent of the sound of water, but the stones smoke, the ground smokes. The path now winds among conical, blackish hills. A petrified landscape. This geometrical severity contrasts with the deliriums that the wind and the rocks conjure up, there ahead on the mountain. The path continues upward for a hundred yards or so, at a not very steep incline, amid heaps of loose stones and coarse gravel. Geometry is succeeded by the formless: it is impossible to tell whether this debris is from the dwellings fallen to ruins or whether it is what remains of rocks that have been worn away, disintegrated by the wind and the sun. The path leads downward once again: weeds, bilious plants, thistles, the stench of cow dung and human and animal filth, rusty tin oil drums full of holes, rags with stains of menstrual blood, a flock of vultures around a dog with its belly ripped to pieces, millions of flies, a boulder on which the initials of the Congress Party have been daubed with tar, the dry bed of the little stream once again, an enormous nim-tree inhabited by hundreds of birds and squirrels, more flat

14

stretches of ground and ruins, the impassioned flight of parakeets, a mound that was perhaps once a cenotaph, a wall with traces of red and black paint (Krishna and his harem of cowherds' wives, royal peacocks, and other forms that are unrecognizable), a marsh covered with lotuses and above them a cloud of butterflies, the silence of the rocks beneath the luminous vibrations of the air, the breathing of the landscape, terror at the creaking of a branch or the sound of a pebble displaced by a lizard (the constant invisible presence of the cobra and that other, equally impalpable presence, which never leaves us, the shadow of our thoughts, the reverse of what we see and speak and are), until finally, again walking along the bed of the same dry stream, one reaches a tiny valley.

Behind, and on either side, the flat-topped hills, the landscape leveled by erosion; ahead, the mountain with the footpath that leads to the great sacred pool beneath the rocks, and from there, via the pilgrim path, to the sanctuary at the summit. Scarcely a trace of the abandoned dwellings remains. Along the path here there are three towering, ancient banyan trees. In the shade of them—or rather: immersed in their depths, hidden in the semidarkness of their bowels, as though they were caves and not trees—are a group of lively children dressed in rags. They are watching over a dozen skinny cows resigned to the martyrdom inflicted on them by the flies and cattle ticks. There are also two kid goats and a multitude of crows. The first band of monkeys makes its appearance. The children throw stones at them. Green and gleaming beneath the steady light, two huge pools of pestilential water. Within a few weeks the water will have evaporated and the pools will be beds of fine dust on which the children and the wind will toss and tumble.

Fixity is always momentary. But how can it *always* be so? If it were, it would not be momentary—or would not be fixity. What did I mean by that phrase? I probably had in mind the opposition between motion and motionlessness, an opposition that the adverb *always* designates as continual and universal: it embraces all of time and applies to every circumstance. My phrase tends to dissolve this opposition and hence represents a sly violation of the principle of identity. I say "sly" because I chose the word *momentary* as an adjectival qualifier of *fixity* in order to tone down the violence of the contrast between movement and motionlessness. A little rhetorical trick intended to give an air of plausibility to my violation of the rules of logic. The relations between rhetoric and ethics are disturbing: the ease with which language can be twisted is worrisome, and the fact that our minds accept these perverse games so docilely is no less cause for concern. We ought to subject language to a diet of bread and

Hanumān, Western India, 17th century.

18

water if we wish to keep it from being corrupted and from corrupting us. (The trouble is that a-diet-of-bread-and-water is a figurative expression, as is the-corruption-of-language-and-its-contagions.) It is necessary to unweave (another metaphor) even the simplest phrases in order to determine what it is that they contain (more figurative expressions) and what they are made of and how (what is language made of? and most important of all, is it already made, or is it something that is perpetually in the making?). Unweave the verbal fabric: reality will appear. (Two metaphors.) Can reality be the reverse of the fabric, the reverse of metaphor—that which is on the other side of language? (Language has no reverse, no opposite faces, no right or wrong side.) Perhaps reality too is a metaphor (of what and/or of whom?). Perhaps things are not things but words: metaphors, words for other things. With whom and of what do word-things speak? (This page is a sack of word-things.) It may be that, like things which speak to themselves in their language of things, language does not speak of things or of the world: it may speak only of itself and to itself. ("Thoughts of a dry brain in a dry season.")* Certain realities cannot be expressed, but, and here I quote from memory, "they are what is manifested in language without language stating it." They are what language

* From "Gerontion" by T. S. Eliot

19

does not say and hence says. (What is embodied in language is not silence, which by definition says nothing, nor is it what silence would say if it were to speak. If it were to cease to be silence, and instead be . . .) What is said in language without language saying it is saying (that is to say?): what is really said (that which makes its appearance between one phrase and another, in that crack that is neither silence nor a voice) is what language leaves unsaid (fixity is always momentary).

To return to my initial observation: by means of a succession of patient analyses and in a direction that is the opposite of that of the normal activity of a speaker, whose function is to produce and construct phrases, whereas here it is a question of taking them apart and uncoupling them (de-constructing them, so to speak) we ought to make our way back upstream against the current, retrace our path, and proceeding from one figurative expression to another, arrive back at the root, the original, primordial word for which all others are metaphors. *Momentary* is a metaphor—for what other word? By choosing it as the adjectival qualifier of fixity, I fell into that frequent confusion whereby spatial properties are attributed to time and temporal properties to space, as when we say "all year long," "the march of time," "the sweep of the minute hand," and other expressions of this sort. If I substitute direct statement for the figurative expression, the result is nonsense or a paradox: fixity is (always) *movement.* Fixity in turn thus proves to be a metaphor. What did I mean by that word? Perhaps this: *that which does not change.* Hence the phrase might have been: that which does not change is (always) movement. This is not satisfactory either however: the opposition between nonchange and movement is not clear, and the ambiguity reappears. Since movement is a metaphor for *change,* the best thing will be to say: nonchange is (always) change. It would appear that I have finally arrived at the desired disequilibrium. Nonetheless, change is not the primordial, original word that I am searching for: it is a form of *becoming.* When *becoming* is substituted for *change,* the relation between the two terms is altered, so that I am obliged to replace nonchange by *permanence,* which is a metaphor for *fixity,* as *becoming* is for *coming-to-be,* which in turn is a metaphor for *time* in all its ceaseless transformations. . . . There is no beginning, no original word: each one is a metaphor for another word which is a metaphor for yet another, and so on. All of them are translations of translations. A transparency in which the obverse is the reverse: fixity is always momentary.

I begin all over again: if it does not make sense to say that fixity is *always* momentary, the same may not be true if I say that it *never* is. This morning's sunlight has fallen uninterruptedly on the motionless surface of the little table made of dark wood that is standing in one

21

corner of the neighbors' patio (it finally has a function in these pages: it is serving me as an example in a dubious demonstration) during the brief period when the cloudy sky cleared: some fifteen minutes, just long enough to demonstrate the falsity of the phrase: fixity is never momentary. Perched on a thin wire of shadow, the silver and olive-colored thrush, itself a tapered shadow transformed into light standing out between and against the various glints of broken shards of bottles set into the top of a wall, at the time of day when reverberations depopulate space, a reflection among other reflections, a momentary sharp brightness in the form of a beak, feathers, and the gleam of a pair of eyes; the gray triangular lizard, coated with a powder so fine that its green tint is scarcely visible, quietly at rest in a crack in another wall on another afternoon in another place: not a variegated stone, but a bit of animal mercury; the coppice of cool green foliage on which, between one day and the next, without forewarning, there appears a flame-colored stain that is merely the scarlet armorial emblem of autumn and that immediately passes through different states, like the bed of coals that glows brightly before dying away, from copper to wine-red and from tawny to scorched brown: at each moment and in each state still the same plant; that butterfly I saw one noon in Kasauli, resting motionless on a sunflower, yellow and black like itself, its wings spread, a very thin sheet of Peruvian gold in which all the sun of the Himalayas might well have been concentrated—they are fixed: not there, but here in my mind, fixed for an instant. Fixity is always momentary.

My phrase is a moment, the moment of fixity in the monologue of Zeno the Eleatic and Hui Shih ("I leave today for Yüeh and I arrive yesterday"). In this monologue one of the terms finally devours the other: either motionlessness is merely a state of movement (as in my phrase), or else movement is only an illusion of motionlessness (as among the Hindus). Therefore we ought not to say either *always* or *never*, but almost always or almost never, merely from time to time or more than is generally supposed and less than this expression might indicate, frequently or seldom, consistently or occasionally, we don't have at our disposal sufficient data to state with certainty whether it is periodic or irregular: fixity (always, never, almost always, almost never, etc.) is momentary (always, never, almost always, almost never, etc.) fixity (always, never, almost always, almost never, etc.) is momentary (always, never, almost always, almost never, etc.) fixity. . . . All this means that fixity never is entirely fixity and that it is always a moment of change. Fixity is always momentary.

 I must make an effort (didn't I say that I would now really go to the very end?), leave the spot with the pools of water, and arrive, some thousand yards farther on, at what I call the Gateway. The children accompany me, offer to act as guides, and beg me for coins. I stop to rest alongside a little tree, take out my pocket knife, and cut a branch off. It will serve me as a walking stick and as a standard. The Gateway is a stretch of wall, tall but not very long, that bears faint traces of black and red paint. The entryway is situated in the center of the wall, and is topped by a great Moorish arch. Above and on either side of the arch are two courses of balconies that call to mind those of Seville or Puebla, Mexico, except that these are made of wood rather than of forged iron. Beneath each balcony there is an empty vaulted niche. The wall, the balconies, and the arch are the remains of what must have been a small palace dating from the end of the eighteenth century,

similar to the many others all over the other side of the mountain.

Near the Gateway is a huge banyan tree that must be very old, to judge from the number of its dangling aerial roots and the intricate tangles in which they descend to the ground from the crown, there to attach themselves firmly, ascend again, jut out, and intertwine, like the lines, cables, and masts of a sailing vessel. But the banyan-sailboat is not rotting away in the stagnant waters of some bay, but here in this sandy soil instead. In its branches the devout have fastened colored ribbons, all of them now faded by the rain and the sun. These discolored bits of cloth give it the pitiful air of a giant swathed in dirty bandages. Leaning against the trunk and resting on a small whitewashed platform is a stone about a foot and a half high; its shape is vaguely human and it is daubed all over with thick, shiny, blood-red paint. At the foot of the figure are yellow petals, ashes, broken earthenware pots and other debris that I am unable to identify. The children leap about and point to the stone, shouting "Hanumān, Hanumān!" On hearing them shouting, a beggar suddenly emerges from the rocks to show me his hands eaten away by leprosy. The next moment another mendicant appears, and then another and another.

I move away, walk through the arch, and enter a sort

The palace of Galta, with traces of red and black paint (photograph by Eusebio Rojas).

26

The sacred pool of the sanctuary of Galta (photograph by Eusebio Rojas).

of little square. To the extreme right, a disorderly perspective of collapsing buildings out of plumb; to the left, a wall that repeats the Gateway on a more modest scale: traces of red and black paint, two courses of balconies, and an entryway topped by a graceful arch that affords a glimpse of a vast courtyard choked with hostile vegetation; across the way, a wide, winding street paved with stones and lined with houses in nearly total ruins. In the center of the street, some hundred yards away from where I am now standing, there is a fountain. Monkeys leap over the wall of the Gateway, scamper across the little square, and climb up onto the fountain. They are soon dislodged by the stones that the children throw at them. I walk toward the fountain. Ahead of me is a building that is still standing, without balconies but with massive wooden doors thrown wide open. It is a temple. Alongside the entrances are various booths with canvas awnings in which a few oldsters are selling cigarettes, matches, incense, sweets, prayers, holy images, and other trinkets and baubles. From the fountain one can glimpse the main courtyard, a vast rectangular space paved in flagstones. It has just been washed down and is giving off a whitish vapor. Around it, beneath a little rooftop supported by pillars, are various altars, like stands at a fair. A few wooden bars separate one altar from another, and each divinity from its worshipers. They are more like cages than altars. Two fat priests, naked from the waist up, appear in the entrance and invite me to come in. I decline to do so.

On the other side of the street is a building in ruins but handsome nonetheless. The high wall once again, the two courses of balconies reminiscent of Andalusia, the arch, and on the other side of the arch a stairway possessed of a certain secret stateliness. The stairway leads to a broad terrace surrounded by architectural features that repeat, on a smaller scale, those of the main archway. The lateral arches are supported by columns carved in random, fantastic shapes. Preceded by the monkeys, I cross the street and walk through the arch. I halt, and after a moment of indecision, begin slowly ascending the stairway. At the other end of the street the children and the priests shout something at me that I do not understand.

If I go on in this direction . . . because it is possible not to, and after having declined the invitation of the two obese priests, I could just as well walk on down the street for some ten minutes, come out in the open countryside, and start up the pilgrim path that leads to the great sacred pool and the hermitage at the foot of the rock. If I go on, I will climb the stairway step by step and reach the great terrace. Ah, here I am, breathing deeply in the center of this open rectangle which offers itself to one's gaze with a sort of logical simplicity. The simplicity, the necessity, the felicity of a perfect rec-

29

tangle beneath the changes, the caprices, the violent onslaughts of the light. A space made of air, in which all forms have the consistency of air: nothing has any weight. At the far side of the terrace is a great niche: again the shapeless stone daubed with fiery red pigment and at its feet the offerings: yellow flowers, ashes from burned incense. I am surrounded by monkeys leaping back and forth: robust males that continually scratch themselves and growl, baring their teeth if anyone approaches them, females with their young hanging from their teats, monkeys that drive other monkeys away, monkeys that dangle from the cornices and balustrades, monkeys that fight or play or masturbate or snatch stolen fruit from each other, gesticulating monkeys with gleaming eyes and tails in perpetual motion, howling monkeys with hairless bright-red buttocks, monkeys, monkeys, hordes of monkeys.

I stamp my feet on the ground, I shout at the top of my lungs, I run back and forth, I brandish the stick that I have cut down in the place with the pools of water and make it sing like a whip, I lash out with it at two or three monkeys who scamper away shrieking, I force my way through the others, I cross the terrace. I enter a gallery with a complicated wooden balustrade running the length of it, the repeated motif of which is a female monster with wings and claws that calls to mind the sphinxes of the Mediterranean (between the balusters and the moldings there appear and disappear the curious faces and the perpetually moving tails of the monkeys that keep cautiously following me at a distance), I enter a room in semidarkness, and despite the fact that I am more or less obliged to grope my way along in the deep shadows I can divine that this enclosed area is as spacious as an audience chamber or a banquet room, and presume that it must have been the main court of the harem or the throne room, I catch a glimpse of palpitating black sacks hanging from the ceiling, a flock of sleeping bats, the air is a heavy, acrid miasma, I go out onto another smaller terrace, how much light there is!, the monkeys reappear at the other end, looking at me from a distance with a gaze in which curiosity is indistinguishable from indifference (they are looking at me from across the distance that separates their being monkeys from my being a man), I am now at the foot of a wall stained with damp patches and with traces of paint, most likely it is a landscape, not that of Galta but another, a green and mountainous one, almost certainly it is one of those stereotyped representations of the Himalayas, yes, these vaguely conical and triangular forms represent mountains, Himalayas with snow-capped peaks, steep crags, waterfalls and moons above a narrow gorge, fairytale mountains where wild beasts, anchorites, and marvels abound, in front of them there rises and falls, swells with pride and humbles itself, a moun-

31

tain that creates and destroys itself, a sea shaken with violent spasms, impotent and boiling with monsters and abominations (the two extremes, as irreconcilable as water and fire: the pure mountain that conceals within its folds the paths to liberation/the impure, trackless sea; the space of definition/that of the indefinable; the mountain and its petrified surge: permanence/the sea and its unstable mountains: movement and its illusions; the mountain that is the very image and likeness of being, a tangible manifestation of the principle of identity, as immobile as a tautology/the sea that endlessly contradicts itself, the sea critical of being and of itself), between the mountain and the sea ethereal space and in the middle of this empty expanse a great dark form: the mountain has ejected a fiery meteor, there is a powerful body hanging suspended above the ocean, it is not the sun: it is the elephant of monkeys, the lion, the bull of simians!, it is swimming vigorously in the ether, stroking with its arms and legs in a smooth rhythm, like a giant frog, its head thrust forward, a prow cleaving the winds and scattering storms, its eyes are two lighthouse beacons that pierce whirlwinds and drill through space turned to stone, its dazzling-white teeth gleam between the red gums and the dark lips: razor-sharp fangs that gnaw away distances, the rigid upraised tail is the mast of this terrifying skiff, the entire body, the color of burning coals, is a furnace of energy flying over the waters, a mountain of seething molten copper, the drops of sweat dripping from its body are a potent rain that falls upon millions of marine and terrestrial wombs (tomorrow there will be a great harvest of monsters and marvels), as the reddish comet parts the sky in two the sea lifts up its millions of arms to grab it and destroy it, huge lascivious serpents and demons of the deep rise from their slimy beds and rush forth to meet it, eager to devour the great monkey, eager to copulate with the chaste simian, to break open his great hermetically sealed jars full of semen accumulated over centuries and centuries of abstinence, eager to broadcast the virile substance to the four points of the compass, to disseminate it, to disperse being, multiply appearances, multiply death, eager to extract his thought and his marrow, to drain him of his last drop of blood, to empty him, squeeze him, suck him dry, to turn him into the clapper of a bell, a hollow shell, eager to burn him, to scorch his tail, but the great monkey keeps advancing, covering space in giant strokes, his shadow plows the waves, his head pierces mineral clouds, he sweeps like a tropical hurricane into the blur of shapeless stains that disfigure this entire end of the wall, representations perhaps of Lankā and its palace, perhaps there is painted here everything that Hanumān did and saw there after hav-

33

ing bounded across the sea in one leap—an indecipherable jumble of lines, strokes, spirals, mad maps, grotesque stories, the discourse of monsoons inscribed on this crumbling wall.

Stains: thickets: blurs. Blots. Held prisoner by the lines, the liane of the letters. Suffocated by the loops, the nooses of the vowels. Nipped by the pincers, pecked by the sharp beaks of the consonants. A thicket of signs: the negation of signs. Senseless gesticulation; a grotesque rite. Plethora becomes hecatomb: signs devour signs. The thicket is reduced to a desert, the babble to silence. Decayed alphabets, burned writings, verbal debris. Ashes. Inchoate languages, larvae, fetuses, abortions. A thicket: a murderous pullulation: a wasteland. Repetitions, you wander about lost amid repetitions, you are merely a repetition among other repetitions. An artist of repetitions, a past master of disfigurations, a maestro of demolitions. The trees repeat other trees, the sands other sands, the jungle of letters is repetition, the stretch of dunes is repetition, the plethora is emptiness, emptiness is a plethora, I repeat repetitions, lost in the thicket of signs, wandering about in the trackless sand, stains on

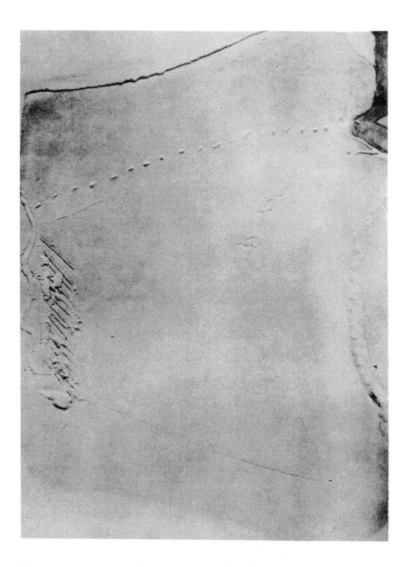

Hanumān, a stone sculpture at the edge of the path to Galta. The devout write out a prayer or trace a sign on a piece of paper and paste it on the stone, which they then cover with red paint (photograph by Eusebio Rojas).

the wall beneath this sun of Galta, stains on this afternoon in Cambridge, a thicket and a stretch of dunes, stains on my forehead that assembles and disassembles vague landscapes. You are (I am) is a repetition among other repetitions. You are is I am; I am is you are: you are is I. Demolitions: I stretch out full length atop my triturations, I inhabit my demolitions.

7

 An indecipherable thicket of lines, strokes, spirals, maps: the discourse of fire on the wall. A motionless surface traversed by a flickering brightness: the shimmer of transparent water on the still bottom of the spring illuminated by invisible reflec-
tors. A motionless surface on which the fire projects silent, fleeting, heaving shadows: beneath the ripples of the crystal-clear water dark phantoms swiftly slither. One, two, three, four black rays emerge from a black sun, grow longer, advance, occupy the whole of space, which oscillates and undulates, they fuse, form once again the dark sun of which they were born, emerge once again from this sun—like the fingers of a hand that opens, closes, and opens once again to transform itself into a fig leaf, a trefoil, a profusion of black wings, before vanishing altogether. A cascade of water silently plunges over the smooth walls of a dam. A charred moon rises out of a gaping abyss. A boat with billowing

sails sends forth roots overhead, capsizes, becomes an inverted tree. Garments that fly in the air above a landscape of hills made of lampblack. Drifting continents, oceans in eruption. Surging waters, wave upon wave. The wind scatters the weightless rocks. A telamon shatters to bits. Birds again, fishes again. The shadows lock in embrace and cover the entire wall. They draw apart. Bubbles in the center of the liquid surface, concentric circles, submerged bells tolling in the depths. Splendor removes her garments with one hand, without letting go of her partner's rod with the other. As she strips naked, the fire on the hearth clothes her in copper-colored reflections. She has dropped her garments to one side and is swimming through the shadows. The light of the fire coils about Splendor's ankles, mounts between her thighs, illuminates her pubis and belly. The sun-colored water wets her fleecy mound and penetrates the lips of her vulva. The tempered tongue of the flames on the moist pudenda; the tongue enters and blindly gropes its way along the palpitating walls. The many-fingered water opens the valves and rubs the stubborn erectile button hidden amid dripping folds. The reflections, the flames, the waves lock in embrace and draw apart. Quivering shadows above the space that pants like an animal, shadows of a double butterfly that opens, closes, opens its wings. Knots. The surging waves rise and fall on Splendor's reclining body. The shadow of an animal drinking in shadows between the parted legs of the young woman. Water : shadow; light: silence. Light: water; shadow: silence. Silence: water; light: shadow.

Stains. Thickets. Surrounded, held prisoner amid the lines, the nooses, the loops of the liane. The eye lost in the profusion of paths that cross in all directions amid trees and foliage. Thickets: threads that knot together, tangled skeins of enigmas. Greenish-black coppices, brambles the color of fire or honey, quivering masses: the vegetation takes on an unreal, almost incorporeal appearance, as though it were a mere configuration of shadows and lights on a wall. But it is impenetrable. Sitting astride the towering wall, he contemplates the dense grove, scratches his bald rump, and says to himself: delight to the eye, defeat of reason. The sun burns the tips of the giant Burmese bamboos, so amazingly tall and slender: their shoots reach to a height of 130 feet and they measure scarcely ten inches in diameter. He moves his head, extremely slowly, from left to right, thus taking in the entire panorama before him, from the giant bamboos to the undergrowth of poisonous trees. As his eyes survey the dense mass, there are

inscribed on his mind, with the same swiftness and accuracy as when letters of the alphabet typed on a machine by skilled hands are imprinted on a sheet of paper, the name and characteristics of each tree and each plant: the betel palm of the Philippines, whose fruit, the betel nut, perfumes the breath and turns saliva red; the doum palm and the nibung, the one a native of the Sudan and the other of Java, both of them supple trees that bend and sway gracefully; the kitul palm, from which the alcoholic beverage known as "toddy" is extracted; the talipot palm: its trunk is a hundred feet tall and four feet wide, and on reaching the age of forty it develops a creamy inflorescence that measures some twenty feet across, whereupon it dies; the guaco, celebrated for its curative powers under the name lignum vitae; the gutta-percha tree, slender and modest; the wild banana, *Musa Paradisiaca*, and the traveler's tree, a vegetable fountain: it stores in the veins of its huge leaves quarts and quarts of potable water that thirsty travelers who have lost their way drink eagerly; the upa-tree: its bark contains ipoh, a poison that causes swelling and fever, sets the blood on fire, and kills; the Queensland shrub, covered with flowers resembling sea anemones, plants that produce dizziness and delirium; the tribes and confederations of hibiscuses and mallows; the rubber tree, confidant of the Olmecs, dripping with sap in the steamy shadows of the forest; the flame-colored mahogany; the okari nut tree, delight of the Papuan; the Ceylon jack, the fleshy brother of the breadfruit tree, whose fruits weigh more than fifty pounds; a tree well known in Sierra Leone: the poisonous sanny; the rambutan of Malaya: its leaves, soft to the touch, hide fruits bristling with spines; the sausage tree; the daluk: its milky sap causes blindness; the bunya-bunya araucaria (better known, he thought with a smile, as the monkey-puzzle tree) and the South American araucaria, a bottle-green cone two hundred feet high; the magnolia of Hindustan, the champak mentioned by Vālmīki on describing the visit of Hanumān to the grove of Ashoka, on the grounds of the palace of Rāvana, in Lankā; the sandalwood tree and the false sandalwood tree; the datura plant, the source of the drug of ascetics; the gum tree, in perpetual tumescence and detumescence; the kimuska, that the English call "flame of the forest," a passionate mass of foliage ranging from bright orange to fiery red, rather refreshing in the dryness of the endless summers; the ceiba and the ceibo, drowsy, indifferent witnesses of the spectacle of Palenque and Angkor; the mamey: its fruit a live coal inside a rugby ball; the pepper plant and its first cousin the terebinth; the Brazilian ironwood tree and the giant orchid of Malaya; the nam-nam and the almond trees of Java, that are not almond trees but huge carved rocks; certain sinister Latin American trees—which I shall not name in

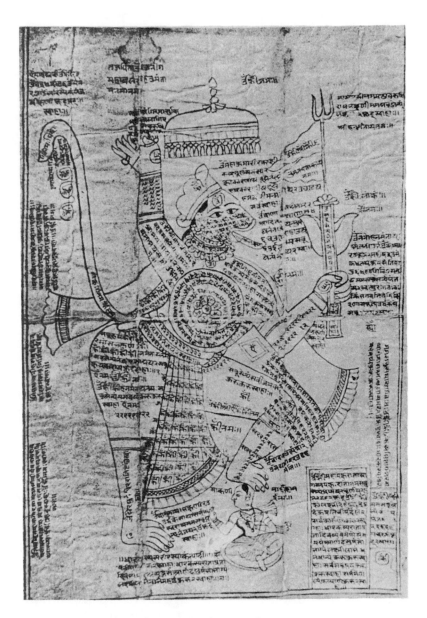

Hanumān, Rajasthan, 18th century.

44

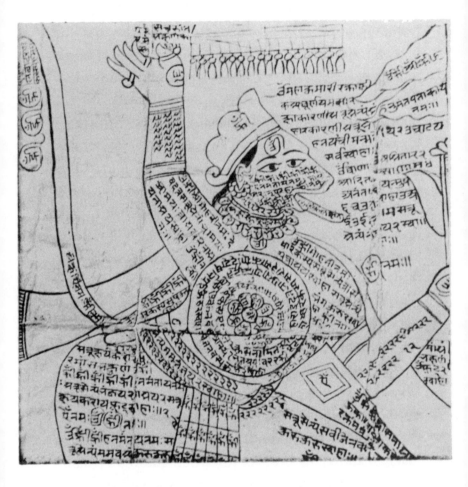

Hanumān, Rajasthan, 18th century: detail.

order to punish them—with fruits resembling human heads that give off a fetid odor: the vegetable world repeats the horror of the shocking history of that continent; the hora, that produces fruits so light that the breezes transport them; the inflexible breakaxe tree; the industrious bignonia of Brazil: it builds suspension bridges between one tree and another, thanks to the hooks with which it climbs and the tendrils with which it anchors itself; the snakewood, another acrobat climber, also skilled in the use of hooks, with markings like a snake skin; the oxypetal coiled up amid blue roots; the balsam fig with its strangling aerial roots; the double coconut palm, thus called because it is bisexual (and also known as the sea coconut since its bilobate or trilobate fruits, enveloped in a huge husk and mindful of huge genital organs, are found floating in the Indian Ocean): the male inflorescence is shaped like a phallus, measures three feet in length, and smells like a rat, whereas the female inflorescence is round, and when artificially pollenized, takes ten years to produce fruit; the goda kaduro of Oceania: its flat gray seeds contain the alkaloid of strychnine; the inkbush, the rain tree; the ombu: a lovely shadow; the baobab; rosewood and the Pernambuco ironwood; ebony; the bo tree, the sacred fig beneath whose shade the Buddha vanquished Mara, a plant that strangles; the aromatic karunbu neti of the

Moluccas, and the amomum that produces the spice known as grains of paradise; the bulu and the twining dada kehel. . . . The Great Monkey closes his eyes, scratches himself again and muses: before the sun has become completely hidden—it is now fleeing amid the tall bamboo trees like an animal pursued by shadows—I shall succeed in reducing this grove of trees to a catalogue. A page of tangled plant calligraphy. A thicket of signs: how to read it, how to clear a path through this denseness? Hanumān smiles with pleasure at the analogy that has just occurred to him: calligraphy and vegetation, a grove of trees and writing, reading and a path. Following a path: reading a stretch of ground, deciphering a fragment of world. Reading considered as a path toward. . . . The path as a reading: an interpretation of the natural world? He closes his eyes once more and sees himself, in another age, writing (on a piece of paper or on a rock, with a pen or with a chisel?) the act in the *Mahanātaka* describing his visit to the grove of the palace of Rāvana. He compares its rhetoric to a page of indecipherable calligraphy and thinks: the difference between human writing and divine consists in the fact that the number of signs of the former is limited, whereas that of the latter is infinite; hence the universe is a meaningless text, one which even the gods find illegible. The critique of the universe (and that of the gods) is called grammar. . . . Disturbed by this strange thought, Hanumān leaps down from the wall, remains for a moment in a squatting position, then stands erect, scrutinizes the four points of the compass, and resolutely makes his way into the thicket.

Phrases that are liane that are damp stains that are shadows projected by the fire in a room not described that are the dark mass of the grove of beeches and aspens lashed by the wind some three hundred yards from my window that are demonstrations of light and shadow based on a vegetable reality at the hour of sunset whereby time in an allegory of itself imparts to us lessons of wisdom which the moment they are formulated are immediately destroyed by the merest flickers of light or shadow which are nothing more than time in its incarnations and disincarnations which are the phrases that I am writing on this paper and that disappears as I read them:

they are not the sensations, the perceptions, the mental images, and the thoughts which flare up and die away here, now, as I write or as I read what I write:

they are not what I see or what I have seen, they are the reverse of what is seen and of the power of sight—but they are not the invisible: they are the unsaid residuum;

they are not the other side of reality but, rather, the other side of language, what we have on the tip of our tongue that vanishes before it is said, the other side that cannot be named because it is the opposite of a name:

what is not said is not this or that which we leave unsaid, nor is it neither-this-nor-that: it is not the tree that I say I see but the sensation that I feel on sensing that I see it at the moment when I am just about to say that I see it, an insubstantial but real conjunction of vibrations and sounds and meanings that on being combined suggest the configuration of a green-bronze-black-woody-leafy-sonorous-silent presence;

no, it is not that either, if it is not a name it surely cannot be the description of a name or the description of the sensation of the name or the name of the sensation:

a tree is not the name tree, nor is it the sensation of tree: it is the sensation of a perception of tree that dies away at the very moment of the perception of the sensation of tree;

names, as we already know, are empty, but what we did not know, or if we did know, had forgotten, is that sensations are perceptions of sensations that die away, sensations that vanish on becoming perceptions, since if they were not perceptions, how would we know that they are sensations?;

sensations that are not perceptions are not sensations, perceptions that are not names—what are they?

if you didn't know it before, you know now: every-thing is empty;

and the moment I say everything-is-empty, I am aware that I am falling into a trap: if everything is empty, this everything-is-empty is empty too;

no, it is full, full to overflowing, everything-is-empty is replete with itself, what we touch and see and taste and smell and think, the realities that we invent and the realities that touch us, look at us, hear us, and invent us, everything that we weave and unweave and everything that weaves and unweaves us, momentary appearances and disappearances, each one different and unique, is always the same full reality, always the same fabric that is woven as it is unwoven: even total emptiness and utter privation are plenitude (perhaps they are the apo-gee, the acme, the consummation and the calm of pleni-tude), everything is full to the brim, everything is real, all these invented realities and all these very real in-ventions are full of themselves, each and every one of them, replete with their own reality;

and the moment I say this, they empty themselves: things empty themselves and names fill themselves, they are no longer empty, names are plethoras, they are do-nors, they are full to bursting with blood, milk, semen, sap, they are swollen with minutes, hours, centuries, pregnant with meanings and significations and signals, they are the secret signs that time makes to itself, names suck the marrow from things, things die on this page but names increase and multiply, things die in order that names may live:

the tree disappears between my lips as I say it and as it vanishes it appears: look at it, a whirlwind of leaves and roots and branches and a trunk amid the violent gusts of wind, a waterspout of green bronze sonorous leafy reality here on the page:

look at it over there, on the slight prominence of that stretch of ground: opaque amid the opaque mass of the trees, look at it, unreal in its brute mute reality, look at it unsaid:

the reality beyond language is not completely reality, a reality that does not speak or say is not reality;

and the moment I say that, the moment I write, letter by letter, that a reality stripped of names is not reality, the names evaporate, they are air, they are a sound encased in another sound and in another and another, a murmur, a faint cascade of meanings that fade away to nothingness:

the tree that I say is not the tree that I see, tree does not say tree, the tree is beyond its name, a leafy, woody reality: impenetrable, untouchable, a reality beyond signs, immersed in itself, firmly planted in its own reality: I can touch it but I cannot name it, I can set fire to it but if I name it I dissolve it:

the tree that is there among the trees is not the tree

Hanumān emerging out of Surasa's mouth. Lucknow, 20th century. Surasa: she-devil.

that I name but a reality that is beyond names, beyond the word reality, it is simply reality just as it is, the abolition of differences and also the abolition of similarities;

the tree that I name is not the tree, and the other one, the one that I do not name and that is there, on the other side of my window, its trunk now black and its foliage still inflamed by the setting sun, is not the tree either, but, rather, the inaccessible reality in which it is planted:

between the one and the other there appears the single tree of sensation which is the perception of the sensation of tree that is vanishing, but

who perceives, who senses, who vanishes as sensations and perceptions vanish?

at this very moment my eyes, on reading what I am writing with a certain haste in order to reach the end (which end? what end?) without having to rise from my chair to turn on the electric light, still taking advantage of the setting sun that is slipping down between the branches and the leaves of the mass of beeches planted on a slight prominence,

(it might be said that this little mound is the pubis of this stretch of ground, so feminine is the landscape between the domes of the little astronomical observatories and the gentle undulations of the playing field of the college, it might be said that it is the pubis of Splendor that grows brighter and then darker, a double butterfly, as the flames on the hearth flicker, as the tide of the night ebbs and flows),

at this very moment my eyes, on reading what I am writing, invent the reality of the person who is writing this long phrase; they are not inventing me, however, but a figure of speech: the writer, a reality that does not coincide with my own reality, if it is the case that I have any reality that I can call my own;

no, no reality is mine, no reality belongs to me (to us), we all live somewhere else, beyond where we are, we are all a reality different from the word I or the word we;

our most intimate reality lies outside ourselves and is not ours, and it is not one but many, plural and transitory, we are this plurality that is continually dissolving, the self is perhaps real, but the self is not *I* or *you* or *he*, the self is neither mine nor yours,

it is a state, a blink of the eye, it is the perception of a sensation that is vanishing, but who or what perceives, who senses?

are the eyes that look at what I write the same eyes that I say are looking at what I write?

we come and go between the word that dies away as it is uttered and the sensation that vanishes in perception—although we do not know who it is that utters the word nor who it is that perceives, although we do know that the self that perceives something that is vanishing also vanishes in this perception: it is only the perception of that self's own extinction,

we come and go: the reality beyond names is not habitable and the reality of names is a perpetual falling to pieces, there is nothing solid in the universe, in the entire dictionary there is not a single word on which to rest our heads, everything is a continual coming and going from things to names to things,

no, I say that I perpetually come and go but I haven't moved, as the tree has not moved since I began to write,

inexact expressions once again: *I began, I write*, who is writing what I am reading?, the question is reversible: what am I reading when I write: *who is writing what I am reading?*

the answer is reversible, the phrases at the end are the reverse of the phrases at the beginning and both are the same phrases

that are liane that are damp spots on an imaginary wall of a ruined house in Galta that are the shadows projected by the fire on a hearth lighted by two lovers that are the catalogue of a tropical botanical garden that are an allegory in a chapter in an epic poem that are the agitated mass of the grove of beeches on the other side of my window as the wind etcetera lessons etcetera destroyed etcetera time itself etcetera,

56

the phrases that I write on this paper are sensations, perceptions, images, etcetera, which flare up and die down here, in front of my eyes, the verbal residuum:

the only thing that remains of the felt, imagined, thought, perceived, and vanished realities, the only reality that these evaporated realities leave behind, a reality that, even though it is merely a combination of signs, is no less real than they are:

the signs are not presences but they configure another presence, the phrases fall into line one after the other on the page and as they advance they open up a path toward a temporarily final end,

the phrases configure a presence that disappears, they are the configuration of the abolition of presence,

yes, it is as though all these presences woven by the configurations of the signs were seeking its abolition in order that there might appear those inaccessible trees, immersed in themselves, not said, that are beyond the end of this phrase,

on the other side, there where eyes read what I am writing, and on reading it, dissipate it

10

 He saw many women lying stretched out on mats, in diverse costumes and finery, their hair adorned with flowers; they had fallen asleep under the influence of the wine, after having spent half the night disporting themselves. And the stillness of that great company, now that their tinkling ornaments had fallen silent, was that of a vast nocturnal pool, covered with lotuses, with no sound now of swans or of bees. . . . The noble monkey said to himself: *Here there have come together planets which, their store of merits having been exhausted, are fallen from the firmament.* It was true: the women glowed like incandescent fallen meteors. Some had collapsed in a heap, fast asleep, in the middle of their dances and were lying as though struck by a bolt of lightning, their hair and headdresses in disarray, amid their scattered garments; others had flung their garlands to the floor, and with the strings of their necklaces broken, their belt buckles unfastened, their skirts thrown

back, looked like unsaddled mares; still others, having lost their bracelets and earrings, with their tunics torn to shreds and trampled underfoot, had the appearance of climbing vines trod upon by wild elephants. Here and there lunar reflections cast by scattered pearls criss-crossed between sleeping swans of breasts. Those women were rivers: their thighs the shores; the undulations of their pubes and bellies ripples of water in the breeze; their haunches and breasts the hills and mounds that the current flows round and girdles; their faces the lotuses; their desires the crocodiles; their sinuous bodies the bed of the stream. On ankles and wrists, forearms and shoulders, round the navel or at the tips of their breasts, there could be seen graceful scratches and pleasing purple bruises that resembled jewels. . . . Some of these girls savored the lips and tongues of their female companions, who returned their kisses as though they were those of their master; their senses awakened though their spirits slumbered, they made love to each other, or lying by themselves, they clung with arms bedecked with jewels to a heap of their own garments, or beneath the domin-ion of wine and desire, some reclined against the belly of a companion or between her thighs, and others rested their head on the shoulder of a neighbor or hid their face between her breasts, and thus they coupled together, each with another, like the branches of a single tree.

These slender women intertwined like flowering vines at the season when they cover the trunks of the trees and open their corollas to the March winds. These women twined together and wound their arms and legs about each other till they formed an intricate sylvan grove. (*Sundara Kund*, IX)

 The transfiguration of their games and embraces into a meaningless ceremony filled them at once with fear and pleasure. On the one hand, the spectacle fascinated them and even excited their lust: that pair of giant lovers were themselves; on the other hand, the feeling of excitement that overcame them on seeing themselves as images of fire was allied with a feeling of anxiety, summed up in a question more apprehensive than incredulous: were they indeed themselves? On seeing those insubstantial forms silently appear and disappear, circle round each other, fuse and split apart, grope at each other and tear each other into bits that vanished and a moment later reappeared in order to form another chimerical body, it seemed to them that they were witnessing not the projection of their own actions and movements but a fantastic spectacle with no relation whatsoever to the reality that they were living at that moment. The ambiguous staging of an endless procession, made up of a succession of

incoherent scenes of adoration and profanation, the climax of which was a sacrifice followed by the resurrection of the victim: yet another avid apparition that opened another scene different from the one that had just taken place, but possessed of the same insane logic. The wall showed them the metamorphosis of the transports of their bodies into a barbarous, enigmatic, scarcely human fable. Their actions were transformed into a dance of specters, this world reborn in the other world: reborn and disfigured: a cortege of bloodless, lifeless hallucinations.

The bodies that are stripped naked beneath the gaze of the other and their own, the caresses that knot them together and unknot them, the net of sensations that traps them and unites them as it disunites them from the world, the momentary bodies that two bodies form in their eagerness to be a single body—all this was transformed into a weft of symbols and hieroglyphs. They were unable to read them: immersed in the passionate reality of their bodies, they perceived only fragments of that other passion depicted on the wall. But even if they had paid close attention to the procession of silhouettes as it passed by, they would not have been able to interpret it. Despite having scarcely seen the cortege of shadows, they nonetheless knew that each one of their gestures and positions was inscribed on the wall, transfigured into a tangled jumble of scorpions or birds, hands or fish, discs or cones, transitory, shifting signs. Each movement engendered an enigmatic form, and each form intertwined with another and yet another. Coils of enigmas which in turn intertwined with others and coupled like the branches of a grove of trees or the tendrils of a creeping vine. In the flickering light of the fire the outlines of the shadows followed one upon the other, linked together in a chain. And just as they did not know the meaning of that theater of signs and yet were not unaware of its dark, passionate theme, so they knew that even though it was composed of mere shadows, the bower formed by its interweaving bodies was impenetrable.

Black clusters hanging from a ragged rock that is indistinct yet powerfully masculine, suddenly cracking asunder like an idol split apart with an axe: bifurcations, ramifications, disintegrations, coagulations, dismemberments, fusions. An inexhaustible flow of shadows and forms in which the same elements kept appearing—their bodies, their garments, the few objects and pieces of furniture in the room—combined each time in a different way, although, as in a poem, there were repetitions, rhymes, analogies, figures that appeared and reappeared with more or less the regularity of a surging sea: beds of lava, flying scissors, violins dangling from a noose, vessels full of seething letters of the alphabet, eruptions of triangles, pitched battles between rectangles and hexagons, thousands of dead victims of the London plague transmuted into clouds on which the Virgin ascends changed into the thousands of naked bodies locked in embrace of one of the colossal orgies of Harmony dreamed of by Fourier turned into the towering flames that devour the corpse of Sardanapalus, seagoing mountains, civilizations drowned in a drop of theological ink, screw propellers planted on the Mount of Calvary, conflagrations, conflagrations, the wind perpetually amid the flames, the wind that stirs up the ashes and scatters them.

Splendor leans back on the mat and with her two hands presses her breasts together but in such a way as to leave, down below, a narrow opening into which her companion, obeying the young woman's gesture of invitation, introduces his rod. The man is kneeling and Splendor's body lies outstretched beneath the arch of his legs, her torso half erect in order to facilitate her partner's thrusts. After a few vigorous assaults the rod traverses the channel formed by the young woman's breasts and reappears in the shadowy zone of her throat, very close to her mouth. She endeavors in vain to caress the head of the member with her tongue: its position prevents her from doing so. With a gesture that is swift but not violent, the man pushes upward and forward, making her breasts bound apart, and his rod emerges from between them like a swimmer returning to the

Hanumān devouring the Sun and being followed by Indra. Alwar, Rajasthan.

surface, in reach now of Splendor's lips. She wets it with her tongue, draws it toward her, and guides it into the red grotto. The man's balls swell. A great splash. Concentric circles cover the surface of the pool. The clapper of the submerged bell tolls solemnly.

On the wall the body of the man is a bridge suspended over a motionless river: Splendor's body. As the crackling of the fire on the hearth diminishes, the shadow of the man kneeling above the young woman increases in size until it covers the entire wall. The conjoining of the shadows precipitates the discharge. Sudden whiteness. An endless fall in a pitch-black cave. Afterwards he discovers himself lying beside her, in a half-shadow on the shore of the world: farther beyond are the other worlds, that of the objects and the pieces of furniture in the room and the other world of the wall, barely illuminated by the faint glow of the dying embers. After a time the man rises to his feet and stirs up the fire. His shadow is enormous and flutters all about the room. He returns to Splendor's side and watches the reflections of the fire glide over her body. Garments of light, garments of water: her nakedness is more naked. He can now see her and grasp the whole of her. Before he had glimpsed only bits and pieces of her: a thigh, an elbow, the palm of a hand, a foot, a knee, an ear nestling in a lock of damp hair, an eye between eyelashes, the softness of backs of knees and insides of thighs reaching up as far as the dark zone rough to the touch, the wet black thicket between his fingers, the tongue between the teeth and the lips, a body more felt than seen, a body made of pieces of a body, regions of wetness or dryness, open or bosky areas, mounds or clefts, never the body, only its parts, each part a momentary totality in turn immediately split apart, a body segmented, quartered, carved up, chunks of ear ankle groin neck breast finger-nail, each piece a sign of the body of bodies, each part whole and entire, each sign an image that appears and burns until it consumes itself, each image a chain of vibrations, each vibration the perception of a sensation that dies away, millions of bodies in each vibration, millions of universes in each body, a rain of universes on the body of Splendor which is not a body but the river of signs of her body, a current of vibrations of sensations of perceptions of images of sensations of vibrations, a fall from whiteness to blackness, blackness to whiteness, whiteness to whiteness, black waves in the pink tunnel, a white fall in the black cleft, never the body but instead bodies that divide, excision and proliferation and dis-sipation, plethora and abolition, parts that split into parts, signs of the totality that endlessly divides, a chain of perceptions of sensations of the total body that fades away to nothingness.

Almost timidly he caresses the body of Splendor with the palm of his hand, from the hollow of the throat to the feet. Splendor returns the caress with the same sense of astonishment and recognition: her eyes and hands also discover, on contemplating it and touching it, a body that before this moment she had glimpsed and felt only as a disconnected series of momentary visions and sensations, a configuration of perceptions destroyed almost the instant it took shape. A body that had disappeared in her body and that at the very instant of that disappearance had caused her own to disappear: a current of vibrations that are dissipated in the perception of their own dissipation, a perception which is itself a dispersion of all perception but which for that very reason, because it is the perception of disappearance at the very moment it disappears, goes back upstream against the current, and following the path of dissolutions, recreates forms and universes until it again manifests itself in a body: this body of a man that her eyes gaze upon.

On the wall, Splendor is an undulation, the reclining form of sleeping hills and valleys. Activated by the fire whose flames leap up again and agitate the shadows, this mass of repose and sleep begins to stir again. The man speaks, accompanying his words with nods and gestures. On being reflected on the wall, these movements create a pantomime, a feast and a ritual in which a victim is quartered and the parts of the body scattered in a space that continually changes form and direction, like the stanzas of a poem that a voice unfolds on the

A sādhu of Galta (photograph by Eusebio Rojas).

moving page of the air. The flames leap higher and the wall becomes violently agitated, like a grove of trees lashed by the wind. Splendor's body is racked, torn apart, divided into one, two, three, four, five, six, seven, eight, nine, ten parts—until it finally vanishes altogether. The room is inundated with light. The man rises to his feet and paces back and forth, hunching over slightly and seemingly talking to himself. His stooping shadow appears to be searching about on the surface of the wall—smooth, flickering, and completely blank: empty water—for the remains of the woman who has disappeared.

12

 On the wall of the terrace the heroic feats of Hanumān in Lankā are now only a tempest of lines and strokes that intermingle with the purplish damp stains in a confused jumble. A few yards farther on, the stretch of wall ends in a pile of debris. Through the wide breach the surrounding countryside of Galta can be seen: straight ahead, bare forbidding hills that little by little fade away into a parched, yellowish expanse of flat ground, a desolate river valley subjected to the rule of a harsh, slashing light: to the left ravines and rolling hills, and on the slopes or at the tops piles of ruins, some inhabited by monkeys and others by families of pariahs, almost all of them members of the Balmik caste (they sweep and wash floors, collect refuse, cart away offal; they are specialists in dust, debris, and excrement, but here, installed amid the ruins and the rubble of the abandoned mansions, they also till the soil on neighboring farms and in the afternoon they gather together in the courtyards and on the terraces to share a

71

hookah, talk together, and tell each other stories); to the right, the twists and turns of the path that leads to the sanctuary at the top of the mountain. A bristling, ocher-colored terrain, sparse thorny vegetation, and scattered here and there, great white boulders polished by the wind. In the bends of the path, standing alone or in groups, powerful trees: pipals with hanging aerial roots, sinewy, supple arms with which for centuries they have strangled other trees, cracked boulders, and demolished walls and buildings; eucalyptuses with striped trunks and aromatic leaves; neem trees with corrugated, mineral-hard bark—in their fissures and forks, hidden by the acrid green of the leaves, there are colonies of tiny squirrels with huge bushy tails, hermit bats, flocks of crows. Imperturbable skies, indifferent and empty, except for the figures delineated by birds: circles and spirals of eaglets and vultures, ink spots of crows and black-birds, green zigzag explosions of parakeets.

The muffled sound of rocks falling into a torrent: the cloud of dust raised by a flock of little black and tan goats led by two young shepherd boys, one of them playing a tune on a mouth organ and the other humming the words. The cool sound of the footsteps, the voices, and the laughter of a band of women descending from the sanctuary, loaded down with children as though they were fruit-bearing trees, barefoot and perspiring, their arms and ankles decked with many jangling bracelets—the dusty, tumultuous throng of women and the brilliant colors of their garments, violent reds and yellows, their coltlike gait, the tinkle of their laughter, the immensity of their eyes. Farther up, some fifty yards beyond the round fortified tower in ruins that once marked the outer limit of the city, invisible from here (one must branch off to the left and go around a huge rock that stands in the way), the terrain becomes more broken: there is a barrier of boulders and at the foot of them a pool surrounded by heterogeneous buildings. Here the pilgrims rest after performing their ablutions. The spot is also a shelter for wandering ascetics. Among the rocks grow two much-venerated pipal trees. The water of the cascade is green, and the roar it makes as it rushes down makes me think of that of elephants at their bathtime. It is six o'clock; at this hour in the late afternoon the *sādhu*, the holy man who lives in some nearby ruins, leaves his retreat and, naked from head to foot, heads for the sacred pool. For years, even in the coldest days of December and January, he has performed his ritual ablutions as dawn breaks and as twilight falls. Although he is over sixty years old, he has the body of a young man and his gaze is clear. After his bath in the late afternoon, he recites his prayers, eats the meal that the devout bring to him, drinks a cup of tea and inhales a few puffs of hashish from his pipe or takes a little bhang in a cup of milk—not in order to stimulate his imagination, he says, but in order to calm it. He is searching for equanimity, the point where the opposition between inner and outer vision, between what we see and what we imagine, ceases. I should like to speak with the sadhu, but he does not understand my language and I do not speak his. Hence I limit myself to sharing his tea, his bhang, and his tranquillity from time to time. What does he think of me, I wonder? Perhaps he is now asking himself the same question, if perchance he thinks of me at all.

I feel someone watching me and turn around: the band of monkeys is spying on me from the other end of the terrace. I walk toward them in a straight line, unhurriedly, my stick upraised; my behavior does not seem to make them uneasy, and as I continue to walk toward them, they remain there, scarcely moving, looking at me with their usual irritating curiosity and their no less usual impertinent indifference. As soon as they feel me close by, they leap up, scamper off, and disappear behind the balustrade. I walk over to the opposite edge of the terrace and from there I see in the distance the bony crest of the mountain outlined with cruel precision. Down below, the street and the fountain, the temple and its two priests, the booths and their elderly vendors, the children leaping about and screeching, several starving cows, more monkeys, a lame dog. Everything is radiant: the animals, the people, the trees,

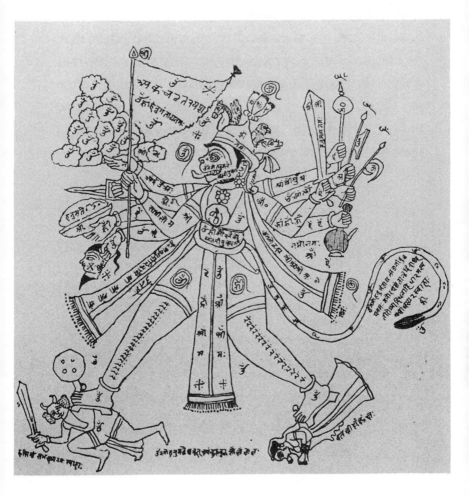

Ten-armed Hanumān, Jodhpur, 19th century.

the stones, the filth. A soft radiance that has reached an accord with the shadows and their folds. An alliance of brightnesses, a thoughtful restraint: objects take on a secret life, call out to each other, answer each other, they do not move and yet they vibrate, alive with a life that is different from life. A universal pause: I breathe in the air, the acrid odor of burned dung, the smell of incense and poverty. I plant myself firmly in this moment of motionlessness: the hour is a block of pure time.

 A thicket of lines, figures, forms, colors: nooses of curving strokes, maelstroms of color in which the eye drowns, a series of intertwined figures, repeated in horizontal bands, that totally confound the mind, as though space were being slowly covered line by line, with letters of the alphabet, each one different and yet related to the following one in the same way, and as though all of them, in their various conjunctions, invariably kept producing the same figure, the same word. Nonetheless, in each case the figure (the word) has a different meaning. Different and the same.

Above, the innocent kingdom of animal copulation. A plain covered with sparse, sunscorched grass, strewn with flowers the size of trees and with trees the size of flowers, bounded in the distance by a narrow red-tinged horizon—almost the trace of a scar that is still fresh: it is dawn or sunset—on which tiny, fuzzy white patches merge or dissolve, vague mosques and palaces that are perhaps clouds. And superimposed on this innocuous landscape, filling it completely with their obsessive, repeated fury, tongue thrust out, gleaming white teeth bared, immense staring eyes, pairs of tigers, rats, camels, elephants, blackbirds, hogs, rabbits, panthers, crows, dogs, donkeys, squirrels, a stallion and a mare, a bull and a cow—the rats as big as elephants, the camels the same size as the squirrels—all coupling, the male mounted atop the female. A universal, ecstatic copulation.

Below: the ground is not yellow or dark gray but a bright parrot-green. Not the earthly kingdom of animals but the meadow-carpet of desire, a brilliant surface dotted with little red, white, and blue flowers, flowers-that-are-stars-that-are-signs (meadow: carpet: zodiac: calligraphy), a motionless garden that is a copy of the fixed night sky that is reflected in the design of the carpet that is transfigured into the pen-strokes of the manuscript. Above: the world in its myriad repetitions; below: the universe is analogy. But it is also exceptions, rupture, irregularity: as in the upper portion, occupying the entire space, outbursts of primal fury, vehement outcries, violent red and white spurts, five in the upper band and four in the lower one, nine enormous flowers, nine planets, nine carnal ideograms: a nāyikā, always the same one, like the repetition of the same luminous patterns in fireworks displays, emerging nine times from the circle of her skirt, a blue corolla spattered with little

78

A monkey of Galta (photograph by Eusebio Rojas).

red dots or a red corolla strewn with tiny black and blue crosses (the sky as a meadow and both reflected in a woman's skirt)—a nāyikā lying on the carpet-garden-zodiac-calligraphy, reclining on a pillow of signs, her head thrown back and half hidden by a translucent veil through which her jet-black, pomaded hair can be seen, her profile transformed into that of an idol by her heavy ornaments—gold earrings set with rubies, diadems of pearls across the forehead, a diamond nose-pendant, chokers and necklaces of green and blue stones—sparkling rivers of bracelets on the arms, breasts with pointed nipples swelling beneath the orange *choli*, the body naked from the waist down, the thighs and belly a gleaming white, the shaved pubis a rosy pink, the labia of the vulva standing out, the ankles circled by bracelets with little tinkling bells, the palms of the hands and the soles of the feet tinted red, the upraised legs clasping the partner nine times—and it is always the same nāyikā, simultaneously possessed nine times in the two bands, five times in the upper one and four in the lower one, by nine lovers: a wild boar, a male goat, a monkey, a stallion, a bull, an elephant, a bear, a royal peacock, and another nāyikā—one dressed exactly like her, with the same jewels and ornaments, the same eyes of a bird, the same great noble nose, the same thick, well-defined mouth, the same face, the same plump whiteness—

another self mounted atop her, a consoling two-headed creature set like a jewel in the twin vulvas.

Asymmetry between the two parts: above, copulation between males and females of the same species; below, copulation of a human female with males of various species of animals and with another human female—never with a human male. Why? Repetition, analogy, exception. On the expanse of motionless space—wall, sky, page, sacred pool, garden—all these figures intertwine, trace the same sign and appear to be saying the same thing, but what is it that they are saying?

14

I halted before a fountain standing in the middle of the street, in the center of a semicircle. The tiny little stream of water flowing from the faucet had made a mud puddle on the ground; a dog with sparse, dark gray fur and patches of raw, bruised flesh was licking at it. (The dog, the street, the puddle: the light of three o'clock in the afternoon, a long time ago, on the cobblestones of a narrow street in a town in the Valley of Mexico, the body of a peasant dressed in white cotton work clothes lying in a pool of blood, the dog that is licking at it, the screams of the women in dark skirts and purple shawls running in the direction of the dead man.) Amid the almost completely ruined buildings forming the semicircle around the fountain was one that was still standing, a massive, squat structure with its heavy doors flung wide open: the temple. From where I was standing its inner courtyard could be seen, a vast quadrangle paved with flagstones (it had

just been washed down and was giving off a whitish vapor). Around the edges of it, against the wall and underneath a roof supported by irregularly shaped pillars, some of stone and others of masonrywork, all of them whitewashed and decorated with red and blue designs, Grecian frets, and bunches of flowers, stood the altars with the gods, separated from each other by wooden bars, as though they were cages. At the entrances were various booths where elderly vendors were peddling their wares to the crowd of worshipers: flowers, sticks and bars of incense; images and color photographs of the gods (depicted by movie actors and actresses) and of Gandhi, Bose, and other heroes and saints; *bhasma,* the soft red paste with which the faithful trace religious signs on their foreheads at the moment in the ceremony when offerings are made; fans with advertisements for Coca-Cola and other soft drinks; peacock feathers; stone and metal lingas; boy dolls representing Durga mounted on a lion; mandarin oranges, bananas, sweets, betel and bhang leaves; colored ribbons and talismans; paperbound prayer books, biographies of saints, little pamphlets on astrology and magic; sacks of peanuts for the monkeys. . . . Two priests appeared at the doors of the temple. They were fat and greasy, naked from the waist up, with the lower part of their bodies draped in a *dhoti,* a length of soft cotton cloth wound between their legs. A Brahman cord hanging down over their breasts, as ample as a wetnurse's; hair, pitch-black and oiled, braided in a pigtail; soft voices, obsequious gestures. On catching sight of me drifting amid the throng, they approached me and invited me to visit the temple. I declined to do so. At my refusal, they began a long peroration, but without stopping to listen to it, I lost myself in the crowd, allowing the human river to carry me along.

The devout were slowly ascending the steep path. It was a peaceful crowd, at once fervent and good-humored. They were united by a common desire: simply to get to where they were going, to see, to touch. Will and its tensions and contradictions played no part in that impersonal, passive, fluid, flowing desire. The joy of total trust: they felt like children in the hands of infinitely powerful and infinitely beneficent forces. The act that they were performing was inscribed upon the calendar of the ages, it was one of the spokes of one of the wheels of the chariot of time. They were walking to the sanctuary as past generations had done and as those to come would do. Walking with their relatives, their neighbors, and their friends and acquaintances, they were also walking with the dead and with those not yet born: the visible multitude was part of an invisible multitude. They were all walking through the centuries by way of the same path, the path that cancels out the distinction between one time and another, and unites the living with the dead. Following this path we leave tomorrow and arrive yesterday: today.

Although some groups were composed only of men or only of women, the majority were made up of entire families, from the great grandparents down to the grandchildren and great grandchildren, and including not only those related by blood but by religion and caste as well. Some were proceeding in pairs: the elderly couples babbled incessantly, but those recently wed walked along without exchanging a word, as though surprised to find themselves side by side. Then there were those walking all by themselves: the beggars with infirmities arousing pity or terror—the hunchbacked and the blind, those stricken with leprosy or elephantiasis or paralysis, those afflicted with pustules or tumors, drooling cretins, monsters eaten away by disease and wasting away from fever and starvation—and the others, erect and arrogant, convulsed with wild laughter or mute and possessed of the bright piercing eyes of illuminati, the sādhus, wandering ascetics covered with nothing but a loincloth or enveloped in a saffron robe, with kinky hair dyed red or scalps shaved bare except for a topknot, their bodies smeared with human ashes or with cow dung, their faces daubed with paint, and carrying in their right

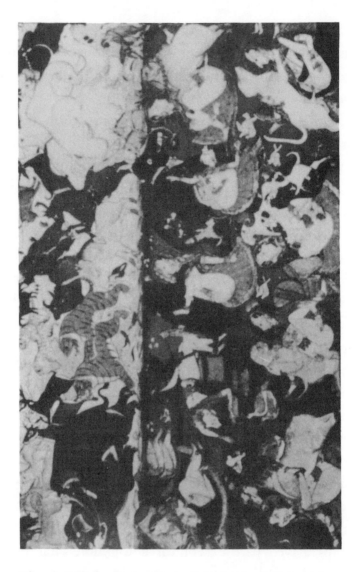

The nāyikā, the incarnation of the love of all creatures, miniature in an album, Rajasthan, c. 1780.

hand a rod in the shape of a trident and in their left hand a tin bowl, their only possession in this world, walking alone or accompanied by a young boy, their disciple, and in certain cases their catamite.

Little by little we crossed hill and dale, amid ruins and more ruins. Some ran ahead and then lay down to rest beneath the trees or in the hollows of the rocks; the others walked along at a slow, steady pace, without halting; the lame and the crippled dragged themselves painfully along, and the invalids and paralytics were borne on stretchers. Dust, the smell of sweat, spices, trampled flowers, sickly-sweet odors, stinking breaths of air, cool breaths of air. Little portable radios, belonging to bands of young boys, poured forth catchy popular love-songs; small children clinging to their mother's breasts or skirts wailed and squalled; the devout chanted hymns; there were some who talked among themselves, some who laughed uproariously, and some who wept or talked to themselves—a ceaseless murmur, voices, cries, oaths, exclamations, outcries, millions of syllables that dissolved into a great, incoherent wave of sound, the sound of humans making itself heard above the other sounds of the air and the earth, the screams of the monkeys, the cawing of the crows, the sea-roar of the foliage, the howl of the wind rushing through the gaps in the hills.

The wind does not hear itself but we hear it; animals communicate among themselves but we humans each talk to ourselves and communicate with the dead and with those not yet born. The human clamor is the wind that knows that it is wind, language that knows that it is language and the means whereby the human animal knows that it is alive, and by so knowing, learns to die. The sound of several hundred men, women, and children walking along and talking: the promiscuous sound of gods, dead ancestors, unborn children and live ones hiding between their mother's bodice and her breast, with their little copper coins and their talismans, their fear of dying. The wind does not complain: man is the one who hears, in the complaint of the wind, the complaint of time. Men hears himself and looks at himself everywhere: the world is his mirror; the world neither hears us nor looks at itself in us: no one sees us, no one recognizes himself in man. To those hills we were strangers, as were the first men who, millennia ago, first walked among them. But those who were walking with me did not know that: they had done away with distance—time, history, the line that separates man from the world. Their pilgrimage on foot was the immemorial rite of the abolishing of differences. Yet these pilgrims knew something that I did not know: the sound of human syllables was simply one more noise amid the other noises of that afternoon. A different sound, yet one identical to the screams of the monkeys, the cries of the parakeets, and the roar of the wind. To know this was to reconcile oneself with time, to reconcile all times with all other times.

15

As he created beings, Prajāpati sweated and suffocated, and from his great heat and fatigue, from his sweat, Splendor was born. She made her appearance all of a sudden: there she was, standing erect, radiant, resplendent, sparkling. The moment they set eyes on her, the gods desired her. They said to Prajāpati: "Allow us to kill her: we can then divide her up and share her among all of us." He answered unto them: "Certainly not! Splendor is a woman: one does not kill women. But if you so wish, you may share her—on condition that you leave her alive." The gods shared her among themselves. Splendor hastened to Prajāpati to complain: "They have taken everything from me!" "Ask them to return to you what they took from you. Make a sacrifice," he counseled her. Splendor had the vision of the offering of the ten portions of the sacrifice. Then she recited the prayer of invitation and the gods appeared. Then she recited the prayer of adoration, backwards, beginning with the

The palace of Galta (18th century), (photograph by Eusebio Rojas).

end, in order that everything might return to its original state. The gods consented to this return. Splendor then had the vision of the additional offerings. She recited them and offered them to the ten. As each one received his oblation, he returned his portion to Splendor and disappeared. Thus Splendor was restored to being.

In this liturgical sequence there are ten divinities, ten oblations, ten restitutions, ten portions of the group of the sacrifice, and the Poem in which it is said consists of stanzas of verses of ten syllables. The Poem is none other than Splendor. (*Satapatha-Brahmana*, 11–4–3)

The word *reconciliation* appears and reappears. For a long time I lighted my way with it, I ate and drank of it. *Liberation* was its sister and its antagonist. The heretic who abjures his errors and returns to the bosom of the church is reconciled with it; the purification of a sacred place that has been profaned is a reconciliation. Separation is a lack, an aberration. A lack: something is missing, we are not whole; an aberration: we have gone astray, we are not in the place where we belong. Reconciliation unites what was separated, it transforms the exclusion into conjunction, it reassembles what has been dispersed: we return to the whole and thus we return to the place where we belong. The end of exile. Liberation opens up another perspective: the breaking of chains and bonds, the sovereignty of free will. Conciliation is dependence, subjection; liberation is self-sufficiency, the plenitude of the one, the excellence of the unique. Liberation: being put to the proof, purgation, purification. When I am alone I am

not alone: I am with myself; being separated is not being excluded: it is being oneself. When with everyone, I am exiled from myself; when I am alone, I am in the whole that belongs entirely to me. Liberation is not only an end of others and of otherness, but an end of the self. The return of the self—not to itself: to what is the same, a return to sameness.

Is liberation the same as reconciliation? Although reconciliation leads by way of liberation and liberation by way of reconciliation, the two paths meet only to divide again: reconciliation is identity in concord, liberation is identity in difference. A plural unity; a selfsame unity. Different, yet the same; precisely one and the same. I am the others, my other selves; I in myself, in selfsameness. Reconciliation passes by way of dissension, dismemberment, rupture, and liberation. It passes by and returns. It is the original form of revolution, the form in which society perpetuates itself and re-engenders itself: regeneration of the social compact, return to the original plurality. In the beginning there was no One: chief, god, I; hence revolution is the end of the One and of undifferentiated unity, the beginning (re-beginning) of variety and its rhymes, its alliterations, its harmonious compositions. The degeneration of revolution, as can be seen in modern revolutionary movements, all of which, without exception, have turned into bureaucratic caesarisms and institutionalized idolatry of the

Chief and the System, is tantamount to the *decomposition* of society, which ceases to be a plural harmony, a *composition* in the literal sense of the word, and petrifies in the mask of the One. The degeneration lies in the fact that society endlessly repeats the image of the Chief, which is nothing other than the mask of *discomposure*: the disconcerting excesses, the imposture of the Caesar. But there never is a one, nor has there ever been a one: each one is an everyone. But there is no everyone: there is always one missing. We are neither a one together, nor is each all. There is no one and no all: there are ones and there are alls. Always in the plural, always an incomplete completeness, the *we* in search of its each one: its rhyme, its metaphor, its different complement.

I felt separated, far removed—not from others and from things, but from myself. When I searched for myself within myself, I did not find myself; I went outside myself and did not discover myself there either. Within and without, I always encountered another. The same self but always another self. My body and I, my shadow and I, their shadow. My shadows: my bodies: other others. They say that there are empty people: I was full, completely full of myself. Nonetheless, I was never in complete possession of myself, and I could never get all the way inside myself: there was always someone else there. Should I do away with him, exorcise him, kill him? The trouble was that the moment that I caught

Hanumān, Kalighat painting (Bengal), 20th century.

sight of him, he vanished. Talk with him, win him over, come to some agreement? I searched for him here and he turned up there. He had no substance, he took up no space whatsoever. He was never where I was; if I was there he was here; if I was here he was there. My invisible foreseeable, my visible unforeseeable. Never the same, never in the same place. Never the same place: outside was inside, inside was somewhere else, here was nowhere. Never anywhere. Great distances away: in the remotest of places: always way over yonder. Where? Here. The other has not moved: I have never moved from my place. He is here. Who is it that is here? *I* am: the same self as always. Where? Inside myself: from the beginning I have been falling inside myself and I still am falling. From the beginning I am always going to where I already am, yet I never arrive at where I am. I am always myself somewhere else: the same place, the other I. The way out is the way in: the way in—but there is no way in, it is all the way out. Here inside is always outside, here is always there, the other always somewhere else. There is always the same: himself: myself: the other. I am that one: the one there. That is how it is; that is what I am.

With whom could I reconcile myself: with myself or with the other—the others? Who were they, who were we? Reconciliation was neither an idea nor a word: it was a seed that, day after day at first and then hour after hour, had continued to grow and grow until it turned into an immense glass spiral through whose arteries and filaments there flowed light, red wine, honey, smoke, fire, salt water and fresh water, fog, boiling liquids, whirlwinds of feathers. Neither a thermometer nor a barometer: a power station that turns into a fountain that is a tree with branches and leaves of every conceivable color, a plant of live coals in winter and a plant of refreshing coolness in summer, a sun of brightness and a sun of darkness, a great albatross made of salt and air, a reflection-mill, a clock in which each hour contemplates itself in the others until it is reduced to nothingness. Reconciliation was a fruit—not the fruit but its maturity, not its maturity but its fall. Reconciliation was an agate planet and a tiny flame, a young girl, in the center of that incandescent marble. Reconciliation was certain colors interweaving so as to form a fixed star set in the forehead of the year, or floating in warm clusters between the spurs of the seasons; the vibration of a particle of light set in the pupil of the eye of a cat flung into one corner of noon; the breathing of the shadows sleeping at the foot of an autumn skinned alive; the ocher temperatures, the gusts of wind the color of dates, a yellowish red, and the green pools of stagnant water, the river basins of ice, the wandering skies dressed in regal rags, the drums of the rain; suns no bigger than a quarter of an hour yet containing all the ages; spiders spinning translucent webs to trap infinitesimal blind creatures that emit light; foliage of flames, foliage of water, foliage of stone, magnetic foliage. Reconciliation was a womb and a vulva, but also the blinks of an eye, provinces of sand. It was night. Islands, universal gravitation, elective affinities, the hesitations of the light that at six o'clock in the late afternoon does not know whether to go or to stay. Reconciliation was not I. It was not all of you, nor a house, nor a past or a future. It was there over yonder. It was not a homecoming, a return to the kingdom of closed eyes. It was going out into the air and saying: *good morning.*

17

 The wall was about two hundred yards long. It was tall, topped with parapets. Save for certain stretches that still showed traces of blue and red paint, it was covered with huge black, green, and dark purple spots: the fingerprints of the rains and the years. Just below the parapets, in a horizontal line running the length of the wall, a series of little balconies could be seen, each one crowned with a dome mindful of a parasol. The wooden blinds were faded and eaten away by the years. Some of the balconies still bore traces of the designs that had decorated them: garlands of flowers, branches of almond trees, little stylized parakeets, seashells, mangoes. There was only one entrance, an enormous one, in the center: a Moorish archway, in the form of a horseshoe. It had once been the elephant gateway, and hence its enormous size was completely out of proportion to the dimensions of the group of buildings as a whole. I took Splendor by the hand and we crossed through the archway together, between the

two rows of beggars on either side. They were sitting on the ground, and on seeing us pass by they began whining their nasal supplications even more loudly, tapping their bowls excitedly and displaying their stumps and sores. With great gesticulations a little boy approached us, muttering something or other. He was about twelve years old, incredibly thin, with an intelligent face and huge, dark, shining eyes. Some disease had eaten away a huge hole in his left cheek, through which one could see some of his back teeth, his gums, and redder still, his tongue, moving about amid little bubbles of saliva—a tiny crimson amphibian possessed by a raging, obscene fit of agitation that made it circle round and round continuously inside its damp grotto. He babbled on endlessly. Although he emphasized his imperious desire to be listened to with all sorts of gestures and gesticulations, it was impossible to understand him since each time he uttered a word, the hole made wheezes and snorts that completely distorted what he was saying. Annoyed by our failure to understand, he melted into the crowd. We soon saw him surrounded by a group of people who began praising his tongue-twisters and his sly ways with words. We discovered that his loquacity was not mere nonsensical babble: he was not a beggar but a poet who was playing about with deformations and decompositions of words.

The main courtyard was a rectangular esplanade that

Hanumān, Rajasthan, 20th century.

had surely been the outdoor "audience chamber," a sort of hall outside the palace itself, although within the walls surrounding it, in which the princes customarily received their vassals and strangers. Its surface was covered with loose dirt; once upon a time it had been paved with tiles the same pink color as the walls. The esplanade was enclosed by walls on three sides: one to the south, another to the east, and another to the west. The one to the south was the Gateway through which we had entered; the other two walls were not as long and not as high. The one to the east was also topped with a parapet, whereas the one to the west had a gable-end roofed over with pink tiles. Like the Gateway, the entryway let into both the other walls was an arch in the form of a horseshoe, although smaller. Along the east wall there was repeated the same succession of little balconies as on the outer face of the Gateway wall, all of them also crowned with parasol domes and fitted out with wooden blinds, most of which had fallen to pieces. On days when the princes received visitors, the women would conceal themselves behind these blinds so as to be able to contemplate the spectacle below without being seen. Opposite the main wall, on the north side of the quadrangle, was a building that was not very tall, with a stairway leading to it which, despite its rather modest dimensions, nonetheless had a certain secret stateliness. The ground floor was nothing more than a massive cube of mortar, with no other function than to serve as a foundation for the upper floor, a vast rectangular hall bordered on all sides by an arcade. Its arches reproduced, on a smaller scale, those of the courtyard, and were supported by columns of random shapes, each one different from the others: cylindrical, square, spiral. The structure was crowned by a great many small cupolas. Time and many suns had blackened them and caused them to peel: they looked like charred, severed heads. From time to time there came from inside them the sound of parakeeets, blackbirds, bats, making it seem as though these heads, even though they had been lopped off, were still emitting thoughts.

The whole was theatrical, mere show. A double fiction: what those buildings represented (the illusions and nostalgias of a world that no longer existed) and what had been staged within their walls (ceremonies in which impotent princes celebrated the grandeur of a power on the point of ceasing to exist). An architecture in which to see oneself living, a substitution of the image for the act and of myth for reality. No, that is not precisely it. Neither image nor myth: the rule of obsession. In periods of decadence obsession is sovereign and takes the place of destiny. Obsession and its fears, its cupidity, its phobias, its monologue consisting of confessions-accusations-lamentations. And it was precisely this, obsession, that redeemed the little palace from its mediocrity and its banality. Despite its mannered hybridism, these courtyards and halls had been inhabited by chimeras with round breasts and sharp claws. A novelistic architecture, at once chivalrous and over-refined, perfumed and drenched with blood. Vividly lifelike and fantastic, chaotic and picturesque, unpredictable. A passionate architecture: dungeons and gardens, fountains and beheadings, an eroticized religion and an esthetic eroticism, the nāyikā's hips and the limbs of the quartered victim. Marble and blood. Terraces, banquet halls, music pavilions in the middle of artificial lakes, bedroom alcoves decorated with thousands of tiny mirrors that divide and multiply bodies until they become infinite. Proliferation, repetition, destruction: an architecture contaminated by delirium, stones corroded by desire, sexual stalactites of death. Lacking power and above all time (architecture requires as its foundation not only a solid space but an equally solid time, or at least capable of resisting the assaults of fortune, but the princes of Rajasthan were sovereigns doomed to disappear and they knew it), they erected edifices that were not intended to last but to dazzle and fascinate. Illusionist castles that instead of vanishing in this air rest on water: architecture transformed into a mere geometric pattern of reflections floating on the surface of a pool, dissipated by the slightest breath of air. . . . There were no pools or musicians on the great

105

esplanade now and no nāyikās were hiding on the little balconies: that day the pariahs of the Balmik caste were celebrating the feast of Hanumān, and the unreality of that architecture and the reality of its present state of ruin were resolved in a third term, at once brutally concrete and hallucinatory.

18

 The grove of trees has turned black and become a gigantic pile of sacks of coal abandoned in the middle of the plot of ground by some unknown person for some unknown reason. A brute reality that says nothing except that it is (but what is it?) and that bears no resemblance to anything at all, not even to those nonexistent sacks of coal with which, ineptly, I have just now compared them. My excuse: the gigantic sacks of coal are as improbable as the grove of trees is unintelligible. Its unintelligibility—a word like a train always just on the point of going off the rails or losing one of its freight cars—stems from its excess of reality. It is a reality irreducible to other realities. The grove of trees is untranslatable: it is itself and only itself. It does not resemble other things or other groves of trees; neither does it resemble itself: each moment it is different. Perhaps I am exaggerating: after all, it is always the same grove of trees and its constant changes do not transform it into either a rock or a

107

locomotive; moreover, it is not unique: the world is full of groves of trees like it. Am I exaggerating though? This grove does indeed resemble others, since otherwise it would not be called a grove of trees but would have another name; yet at the same time its reality is unique and would really deserve to have a proper name. Everyone deserves (we all deserve) a proper name and no one has one. No one has ever had one and no one ever will have one. This is our real eternal damnation, ours and the world's. And this is what Christians mean when they speak of the state of "fallen nature." Paradise is governed by an ontological grammar: things and beings are its names and each name is a proper name. The grove of trees is not unique since it has a name that is a common noun (it is a fallen nature), but at the same time it is unique since it has no name that really belongs to it (it is innocent nature). This contradiction defies Christianity and dashes its logic to bits.

The fact that the grove of trees has no name, not the fact that I see it from my window, as the afternoon draws to a close, a blur against the bold sky of early autumn, a stain that little by little creeps across this page and covers it with letters that simultaneously describe it and conceal it—the fact that it does not have a name and the fact that *it can never have one*, is what impels me to speak of it. The poet is not one who names things, but one who dissolves their names, one who discovers that

Garuda, watercolor, Rajasthan, 19th century.

109

things do not have a name and that the names that we call them are not theirs. The critique of paradise is called language: the abolition of proper names; the critique of language is called poetry: names grow thinner and thinner, to the point of transparency, of evaporation. In the first case, the world becomes language; in the second, language is transformed into a world. Thanks to the poet, the world is left without names. Then, for the space of an instant, we can see it precisely as it is—an *adorable azure*. And this vision overwhelms us, drives us mad; if things are but have no name: *on earth there is no measure whatsoever*.

A moment ago, as it was burning in the solar brazier, the grove of trees did not appear to be an unintelligible reality but an emblem, a configuration of symbols. A cryptogram neither more nor less indecipherable than the enigmas that fire inscribes on the wall with the shadows of two lovers, the tangle of trees that Hanumān saw in the garden of Rāvana in Lankā and that Vālmīki turned into a fabric woven of names that we now read as a fragment of the *Rāmāyana*, the tattoo of monsoons and suns on the wall of the terrace of that small palace in Galta or the painting that describes the bestial and lesbian couplings of the nāyikā as an exception to (or an analogy of?) universal love. The transmutation of forms and their changes and movements into motionless signs: writing; the dissipation of the signs: reading. Through writing we abolish things, we turn them into meaning; through reading, we abolish signs, we extract the meaning from them, and almost immediately thereafter, we dissipate it: the meaning returns to the primordial stuff. The grove does not have a name and these trees are not signs: they are trees. They are real and they are illegible. Although I refer to them when I say: *these trees are illegible*, they do not think of themselves as being referred to. They do not express anything, they do not signify: they are merely there, merely being. I can fell them, burn them, chop them up, turn them into masts, chairs, boats, houses, ashes; I can paint them, carve them, describe them, transform them into symbols of this or of that (even symbols of themselves), and make another grove of trees, real or imaginary, with them; I can classify them, analyze them, reduce them to a chemical formula or a mathematical equation and thus translate them, transform them into language—but *these* trees, the ones that I point to, the ones that are over there just beyond, always just beyond, my signs and my words, untouchable unreachable impenetrable, are what they are, and no name, no combinations of signs says them. They are unrepeatable: they will never again be what they are at this moment.

The grove is already part of the night. Its darkest, most nightlike part. So much so that I write, with no compunction, that it is a pile of coal, a sharp-pointed

Hanumān, drawing on paper, Rajasthan, 19th century.
(J. C. Ciancimino Collection.)

geometry of shadows surrounded by a world of vague ashes. It is still light in the neighbors' patio. An impersonal, posthumous light, for which the word *fixity* is most appropriate, even though we know that it will last for only a few short minutes, because it is a light that seems to resist the ceaseless change of things and of itself. The final, impartial clarity of this moment of transparency in which things become presences and coincide with themselves. It is the end (a provisory, cyclical end) of metamorphoses. An apparition: on the square cement blocks of the patio, astonishingly itself, without ostentation and without diffidence, the dark wooden table on top of which (as I only now discover) there is visible, on one corner, an oval spot with tiger markings, thin reddish stripes. In the opposite corner, the garbage can with the lid half open burns with a quiet, almost solid glow. The light runs down the brick wall as though it were water. A burned water, a water-that-is-fire. The garbage can is overflowing with rubbish and it is an altar that is consuming itself in silent exaltation: the refuse is a sheaf of flames beneath the coppery gleam of the rusty cover. The transfiguration of refuse—no, not a transfiguration: a revelation of garbage as what it really is: garbage. I cannot say "glorious garbage" because the adjective would defile it. The little dark wooden table, the garbage can: presences. Without a name, without a history, without a meaning, without a practical use: just because.

Things rest upon themselves, their foundation is their own reality, and they are unjustifiable. Hence they offer themselves to our sight, touch, hearing, taste, smell—not to our powers of thought. Not to think; to see, rather, to make of language a transparency. I see, I hear the footsteps of the light in the patio: little by little it withdraws from the wall opposite, projects itself onto the one on the left and covers it with a translucent mantle of barely perceptible vibrations: a transubstantiation of brick, a combustion of stone, an instant of incandescence of matter before it flings itself into its blindness—into its reality. I see, I hear, I touch the gradual petrification of language that no longer signifies but merely says: table, garbage can, without really saying them, as the table and the garbage can disappear in the patio that is now totally dark. . . . The night is my salvation. We cannot *see* without risking going mad: things reveal us, without revealing anything, simply by being there in front of us, the emptiness of names, the incommensurability of the world, its quintessential muteness. And as the night accumulates in my window, I feel that I am not from here, but from there, from that world that has just been obliterated and is now awaiting the resurrection of dawn. I come from there, all of us come from there, and we shall one day return there. The fascination held for us by this other face, the seduction of this nonhuman side of the universe: where there is no name, no measure. Each individual, each thing, each instant: a unique, incomparable, incommensurable reality. To return, then, to the world of proper names.

 a rose and green, yellow and purple undulation, wave upon wave of women, a surf of tunics dotted with little bits of mirrors like stars or spangled with sequins, the continual flowering of the pinks and blues of turbans, these thin long-shanked men are flamingos and herons, the sweat runs down the basalt of the cheekbones in rivers, wetting their mustaches that curve dangerously upward like the horns of an attacking bull, making the metal hoops they are wearing in their ears gleam, men with grave eyes as deep as a well, the flutter of feminine fabrics, ribbons, gauzes, transparencies, secret folds that conceal gazes, the tinkle of bracelets and anklets, the swaying of hips, the bright flash of earrings and amulets made of bits of colored glass, clusters of old men and old women and children driven along by the violent gust of wind of the feast-day, devotees of Krishna in pale green skirts, with flowers in their hair and huge dark circles under their eyes,

roaring with laughter, the main courtyard seethed with sounds, smells, tastes, a gigantic basket filled to overflowing with bright yellow, ocher, pomegranate, cinnamon, purple, black, wrinkled, transparent, speckled, smooth, glistening, spiny fruits, flaming fruits, cool refreshing suns, human sweat and animal sweat, incense, cinnamon, dung, clay and musk, jasmine and mango, sour milk, smells and tastes, tastes and colors, betel nut, clove, quicklime, coriander, rice powder, parsley, green and red peppers, honeysuckle, fetid pools, burned cow dung, limes, urine, sugarcane, spit bleeding from betel, slices of watermelon, pomegranates and their little cells: a monastery of blood; guavas, little caverns of perfume; peals of laughter, spilled whitenesses, ivory ceremonial rattles and exclamations, sighs of woe is me and shouts of get a move on, gongs and tambourines, the rustle of leaves of the women's skirts, the pattering rain of the naked feet on the dust, laughter and laments: the roar of water flinging itself over a precipice, the bound and rebound of cries and songs, the mingled chatter of children and birds, childgabble and birdprattle, the prayers of the beggargrims, the driveling supplications of the pilgrim-mendicants, the glug-glug of dialects, the boiling of languages, the fermentation and effervescence of the verbal liquid, gurgling bubbles that rise from the bottom of the Babelic broth and burst on reaching the

A mendicant (sādhu) dressed up as Hanumān at a fair in Ram-tirth at Amritsar.

air, the multitude and its surging tides, its multisurges and its multitudes, its multivalanche, the multisun beating down on the sunitude, povertides beneath the sunalanche, the suntide in its solity, the sunflame on the poverlanche, the multitidal solaritude

 A quiet brightness projects itself on the wall across the way. Doubtless my neighbor has gone upstairs to his study, turned on the lamp next to the window, and by its light is peacefully reading *The Cambridge Evening News*. Down below, at the foot of the wall, the little pure-white daisies peep out of the darkness of the blades of grass and other tiny plants on the miniature meadow. Paths traveled by creatures smaller than an ant, castles built on a cubic millimeter of agate, snowdrifts the size of a grain of salt, continents drifting in a drop of water. The space beneath the leaves and between the infinitesimal plant stems of the meadow teems with a tremendous population continually passing over from the vegetable kingdom to the animal and from the animal to the mineral or the fantastic. That tiny branch that a breath of air faintly stirs was just a moment ago a ballerina with breasts like a top and a forehead pierced by a ray of light.

A prisoner in the fortress created by the lunar reflections of the nail of the little finger of a small girl, a king has been dying in agony for a million seconds now. The microscope of fantasy reveals creatures different from those of science but no less real; although these are visions of ours, they are also the visions of a third party: someone is looking at them (is looking at himself?) through our eyes.

I am thinking of Richard Dadd, spending nine years, from 1855 to 1864, painting *The Fairy-Feller's Masterstroke* in the madhouse at Broadmoor, England. A fairly small painting that is a minute study of just a few square inches of ground—grasses, daisies, berries, tendrils of vines, hazelnuts, leaves, seeds—in the depths of which there appears an entire population of minuscule creatures, some of them characters from fairy tales and others who are probably portraits of Dadd's fellow inmates and of his jailers and keepers. The painting is a spectacle: the staging of the drama of the supernatural world in the theater of the natural world. A spectacle that contains another, a paralyzing and anxiety-filled one, the theme of which is expectation: the figures that people the painting are awaiting an event that is about to take place at any moment now. The center of the composition is an empty space, the point of intersection of all sorts of powers and the focal point on which all eyes are

Detail of The Fairy-Feller's Masterstroke.

Opposite: The Fairy-Feller's Masterstroke, oil by Richard Dadd, 1855-1864 (Tate Gallery, London, photograph courtesy the gallery).

123

trained, a clearing in the forest of allusions and enigmas; in the center of this center there is a hazelnut on which the stone axe of the woodcutter is about to fall. Although we do not know what is hidden inside the hazelnut, we know that if the axe splits it in two, everything will change: life will commence to flow once more and the curse that has turned the figures in the painting to stone will be broken. The woodcutter is a robust young man, dressed in coarse cotton (or perhaps leather) work clothes and wearing on his head a cap from which there tumble locks of curly, reddish hair. With his feet firmly planted on the stony ground, he is grasping, with both hands, an upraised axe. Is this Dadd? How can we tell, since we can see the figure only from the back? Although it is impossible to be certain, I cannot resist the temptation to identify the figure of the woodcutter as being the painter. Dadd was shut up in the insane asylum because during an outing in the country, in a violent fit of madness, he hacked his father to death with an axe. The woodcutter is readying himself to repeat the act, but the consequences of this symbolic repetition will be precisely the contrary of those that resulted from the original act; in the first instance, incarceration and petrification; in the second, on splitting the hazelnut apart, the woodcutter's axe breaks the spell. One disturbing detail: the axe that is about to put an end to the evil spell of petrification is a stone axe. Sympathetic magic.

We are able to see the faces of all the other figures. Some of them peek out of cracks and crevices in the ground and others form a mesmerized circle around the fateful hazelnut. Each of them is rooted to the spot as though suddenly bewitched and all of them create between them a space that is totally empty yet magnetized, the fascination of which is immediately felt by anyone contemplating the painting. I said *felt* when I should have said anticipated, for this space is a place where an apparition is imminent. And for that very reason it is, at one and the same time, absolutely empty and magnetized: nothing is *happening* except anticipation. The figures are rooted to the spot, and both literally and figuratively, they are plants and stones. Anticipation has immobilized them—the anticipation that does away with time but not anxiety. The anticipation is *eternal*: it abolishes time; the anticipation is *momentary*, an awaiting of what is imminent, what is about to happen from one moment to the next: it speeds up time. Fated to await the masterstroke of the woodcutter, the fairies gaze endlessly at a clearing in the forest that is nothing more than the focal point of their gaze and in which nothing whatsoever is happening. Dadd has painted the vision of the act of vision, the look that looks at a space in which the object looked at has been annihilated. The axe which, when it falls, will break the spell that paralyzes them, will never fall. It is an event that is always about to happen and at the same time will never happen. Between *never* and *always* there lies in wait anxiety, with its thousand feet and its single eye.

21

In the rough and trackless stretches of the way to Galta the *Monkey Grammarian* appears and disappears: the monogram of the Simian lost amid his similes.

 No painting can tell a story because nothing happens in it. Painting confronts us with fixed, unchangeable, motionless realities. In no canvas, not even excepting those that have as their theme real or supernatural happenings and those that give us the impression or the sensation of movement, does anything *happen*. In paintings things simply *are*; they do not *happen*. To speak and to write, to tell stories and to think, is to experience time elapsing, to go from one place to another: to advance. A painting has spatial limits, yet it has neither a beginning nor an end; a text is a succession that begins at one point and ends at another. To write and to speak are to trace a path: to create, to remember, to imagine a trajectory, to go toward. . . . Painting offers us a vision, literature invites us to seek one and therefore traces an imaginary path toward it. Painting constructs presences, literature emits meanings and then attempts to catch up with them. Meaning is what words emit, what is beyond them, what escapes

The palace of Galta (photograph by Eusebio Rojas).

from between the meshes of the net of words and what they seek to retain or to trap. Meaning is not in the text but outside it. These words that I am writing are setting forth in search of their meaning, and that is the only meaning they have.

Hanumān: a monkey/a *gramma* of language, of its dynamism and its endless production of phonetic and semantic creations. An ideogram of the poet, the master/servant of universal metamorphosis: an imitative simian, an artist of repetitions, he is the Aristotelian animal that copies from nature but at the same time he is the semantic seed, the bomb-seed that is buried in the verbal subsoil and that will never turn into the plant that its sower anticipates, but into another, one forever different. The sexual fruits and the carnivorous flowers of otherness sprout from the single stem of identity.

24

 Is it vision that lies at the end of the road? The neighbors' patio with its little dark wooden table and its rusty garbage can, the grove of beech trees on a prominence of the playing field of Churchill College, the spot with the pools of stagnant water and the banyan trees a hundred yards or so from what was once the entrance to Galta, are visions of reality irreducible to language. Each one of these realities is unique and to truly express it we would require a language composed solely of proper and unrepeatable names, a language that would not be a language: the double of the world, that would be neither a translation of it nor a symbol of it. Thus seeing these realities, truly seeing them, is the same as going mad: losing all names, entering the realm of the incommensurable. Or rather: returning to it, to the world before language exists. Hence the path of poetic writing leads to the abolition of writing: at the end of it we are confronted with an inexpressible reality. The reality that poetry reveals and

that appears behind language—the reality visible only through the destruction of language that the poetic act represents—is literally intolerable and maddening. At the same time, without the vision of this reality man is not man, and language is not language. Poetry gives us sustenance and destroys us, it gives us speech and dooms us to silence. It is the necessarily momentary perception (which is all that we can bear) of the incommensurable world which we one day abandon and to which we return when we die. Language sinks its roots into this world but transforms its juices and reactions into signs and symbols. Language is the consequence (or the cause) of our exile from the universe, signifying the distance between things and ourselves. At the same time it is our recourse against this distance. If our exile were to come to an end, language would come to an end: language, the measure of all things, *ratio*. Poetry is number, proportion, measure: language—except that it is a language that has turned in upon itself, that devours itself and destroys itself in order that there may appear what is other, what is without measure, the dizzying foundation, the unfathomable abyss out of which measure is born. The reverse of language.

Writing is a search for the meaning that writing itself violently expels. At the end of the search meaning evaporates and reveals to us a reality that literally is meaningless. What remains? The twofold movement of writing: a journey in the direction of meaning, a dissipation of meaning. An allegory of mortality: these phrases that I write, this path that I invent as I endeavor to describe the path that leads to Galta, become blurred, dissolve as I write: I never reach the end, and I never shall. There is no end, everything has been a perpetual beginning all over again. What I am saying is a continual saying of what I am about to say and never manage to say: I always say something else. A saying of something that the moment it is said evaporates, a saying that never says what I want to say. As I write, I journey toward meaning: as I read what I write, I blot it out, I dissolve the path. Each attempt I make ends up the same way: the dissolution of the text in the reading of it, the expulsion of the meaning through writing. The search for meaning culminates in the appearance of a reality that lies beyond the meaning and that disperses it, destroys it. We proceed from a search for meaning to its destruction in order that a reality may appear, a reality which in turn disappears. Reality and its radiance, reality and its opacity: the vision that poetic writing offers us is that of its dissolution. Poetry is empty, like the clearing in the forest in Dadd's painting: it is nothing but the *place* of the apparition which is, at the same time, that of its disappearance. *Rien n'aura lieu que le lieu.*

On the square-ruled wall of the terrace the damp stains and the traces of red, black, and blue paint create imaginary atlases. It is six in the afternoon. A pact between light and shadow: a universal pause. I breathe deeply: I am in the center of a time that is fully rounded, as full of itself as a drop of sunlight. I feel that ever since I was born, and even before, a before that has no when, I have been able to see the banyan tree at the corner of the esplanade growing taller and taller (a fraction of an inch each year), multiplying its aerial roots, interweaving them, descending to the earth by way of them, anchoring itself, taking root, rising again, descending again, and thus, for centuries, growing larger in a tangle of roots and branches. The banyan tree is a spider that has been spinning its interminable web for a thousand years. Discovering this causes me to feel an inhuman joy: I am rooted in this hour as the banyan tree is rooted in time immemorial.

Nonetheless time does not stop: for more than two hours now Splendor and I have been walking through the great arch of the Gateway, crossing the deserted courtyard, and climbing the stairway that leads to this terrace. Time goes by yet does not go by. This hour of six in the afternoon has been, from the beginning, the same six o'clock in the afternoon, and yet minutes follow upon minutes with the same regularity as always. This hour of six in the afternoon little by little draws to a close, but each moment is transparent, and by the very fact of this transparency dissolves or becomes motionless, ceasing to flow. Six o'clock in the afternoon turns into a transparent immobility that has no depth and no reverse side: there is nothing behind it.

The notion that the very heart of time is a fixity that dissolves all images, all times, in a transparency with no depth or consistency, terrifies me. Because the present also becomes empty: it is a reflection suspended in another reflection. I search about for a reality that is less dizzying, a presence that will rescue me from this abysmal now, and I look at Splendor—but she is not looking at me: at this moment she is laughing at the gesticulations of a little monkey as it leaps from its mother's shoulder to the balustrade, swings by its tail from one of the balusters, takes a leap, falls at our feet a few steps away from us, looks up at us in terror, leaps again and this time lands on the shoulder of its mother, who

Hanumān flying over the mountains, Jaipur, 19th century.

growls and bares her teeth at us. I look at Splendor and through her face and her laugh I am able to make my way to another moment of another time, and there on a Paris street corner, at the intersection of the rue du Bac and the rue de Montalembert, I hear the same laugh. And this laugh is superimposed on the laugh that I hear here, on this page, as I make my way inside six o'clock in the afternoon of a day that I am creating and that has stopped still on the terrace of an abandoned house on the outskirts of Galta.

The times and the places are interchangeable: the face that I am now looking at, the one that, without seeing me, laughs at the monkey and its panic, is the one that I am looking at in another city, at another moment—on this same page. Never is the same when, the same laugh, the same stains on the wall, the same light of the same six o'clock in the afternoon. Each when goes by, changes, mingles with other whens, disappears and re-appears. This laughter that scatters itself about here like the pearls of a broken necklace is the same laugh as always and always another, the laugh heard on a Paris street corner, the laugh of an afternoon that is drawing to a close and blending with the laugh that silently, like a purely visual cascade, or rather an absolutely mental one—not the idea of a cascade but a cascade become idea—plunges down onto my forehead and forces me to close my eyes because of the mute violence of its whiteness. Laughter: cascade: foam: unheard whiteness. Where do I hear this laughter, where do I see it? Having lost my way amid all these times and places, have I lost my past, am I living in a continuous present? Although I haven't moved, I feel that I am coming loose from myself: I am where I am and at the same time I am not where I am. The strangeness of being here, as though here were somewhere else; the strangeness of being in my body, of the fact that my body is my body and that I think what I think, hear what I hear. I am wandering far, far away from myself, by way of here, journeying along this path to Galta that I am creating as I write and that dissipates on being read. I am journeying by way of this here that is not outside and yet is not inside either; I am walking across the uneven, dusty surface of the terrace as though I were walking inside myself, but this inside of myself is outside: I see it, I see myself walking in it. "I" is an outside. I am looking at Splendor and she is not looking at me: she is looking at the little monkey. She too is coming loose from her past, she too is in her outside. She is not looking at me, she is laughing, and with a toss of her head, she makes her way inside her own laughter.

From the balustrade of the terrace I see the courtyard below. There is no one there, the light has stopped moving, the banyan tree has firmly planted itself in its immobility, Splendor is standing at my side laughing, the little monkey is terrified and runs to hide in its mother's hairy arms, I breathe in this air as insubstantial as time. Transparency: in the end things are nothing but their visible properties. They are as we see them, they are what we see and I exist only because I see them. There is no other side, there is no bottom or crack or hole: everything is an adorable, impassible, abominable, impenetrable surface. I touch the present, I plunge my hand into the now, and it is as though I were plunging it into air, as though I were touching shadows, embracing reflections. A magic surface, at once insubstantial and impenetrable: all these realities are a fine-woven veil of presences that hide no secret. Exteriority, and nothing else: they say nothing, they keep nothing to themselves, they are simply there, before my eyes, beneath the not too harsh light of this autumn day. An indifferent state of existence, beyond beauty and ugliness, meaning and meaninglessness. The intestines spilling out of the belly of the dog whose body is rotting over there some fifty yards away from the banyan tree, the moist red beak of the vulture ripping it to pieces, the ridiculous movement of its wings sweeping the dust on the ground, what I think and feel on seeing this scene from the balustrade, amid Splendor's laughter and the little monkey's panic—these are distinct, unique, absolutely real realities, and yet they are also inconsistent, gratuitous, and in some way unreal. Realities that have no weight, no reason for being: the dog could be a pile of stones, the vulture a man or a horse, I myself a chunk of stone or another vulture, and the reality of this six o'clock in the afternoon would be no different. Or better put: *different* and *the same* are synonyms in the impartial light of this moment. Everything is the same and it is all the same whether I am who I am or someone different from who I am. On the path to Galta that always begins over and over again, imperceptibly and without my consciously willing it, as I kept walking along it and kept retracing my steps, again and again, this now of the terrace has been gradually constructed: I am riveted to the spot here, like the banyan tree trapped by its populace of intertwining aerial roots, but I might be there, in another now—that would be the same now. Each time is different; each place is different and all of them are the same place, they are all the same. Everything is now.

The path is writing and writing is a body and a body is bodies (the grove of trees). Just as meaning appears beyond writing, as though it were the destination, the end of the road (an end that ceases to be an end the moment we arrive there, a meaning that vanishes the moment we state it), so the body first appears to our eye as a perfect totality, and yet it too proves to be intangible: the body is always somewhere beyond the body. On touching it, it divides itself (like a text) into portions that are momentary sensations: a sensation that is a perception of a thigh, an earlobe, a nipple, a fingernail, a warm patch of groin, the hollow in the throat like the beginning of a twilight. The body that we embrace is a river of metamorphoses, a continual division, a flowing of visions, a quartered body whose pieces scatter, disperse, come back together again with the intensity of a flash of lightning hurtling toward a white black white fixity. A fixity that is destroyed in another black white black flash; the body is the place

marking the disappearance of the body. Reconciliation with the body culminates in the annihilation of the body (the meaning). Every body is a language that vanishes at the moment of absolute plenitude; on reaching the state of incandescence, every language reveals itself to be an unintelligible body. The word is a disincarnation of the world in search of its meaning; and an incarnation: a destruction of meaning, a return to the body. Poetry is corporeal: the reverse of names.

a rose and green, yellow and purple undulation, human tides, whitecaps of light on skin and hair, the inexhaustible flow of the human current that little by little, in less than an hour, inundated the entire courtyard. Leaning on the balustrade, we saw the pulse of the multitude throbbing, heard its swelling surge. A coming and going, a calm agitation that propagated itself and spread in eccentric waves, slowly filled the empty spaces, and as though it were an overflowing stream, mounted, patiently and persistently, step by step, the great stairway of the cubical building, partially in ruins, situated at the north corner of the parallelogram.

On the third and uppermost story of that massive structure, at the top of the stairway and below one of the arches crowning the building, the altar of Hanumān had been erected. The Great Monkey was represented by a relief carved in a block of black stone more than three feet high, approximately thirty inches wide, and half an inch thick, placed on, or rather, set into a platform of modest dimensions covered with a red and yellow cloth. The stone stood beneath a wooden canopy shaped like a fluted conch shell, painted gold. From the conch there hung a length of violet silk with fringes, also gilded, at the bottom. Two poles, mindful of wooden masts, stood on either side of the canopy, both of them painted blue and each of them bearing a triangular paper banner, one of them a green one and the other a white one. Scattered about on the bright red and yellow cloth covering the table of the altar were little piles of ashes from incense burned in honor of the image, and many petals, still fresh and moist, the remains of the floral offerings of the faithful. The stone was smeared with a brilliant red paste. Bathed in the lustral water, the nectar of the flowers and the melted butter of the oblations, the relief of Hanumān gleamed like the body of an athlete anointed with oil. Despite the thick red pigment, one could more or less make out the figure of the Simian, taking that extraordinary leap that brought him from the Nilgiri Mountains to the garden of the palace of Rāvana in Lankā; his left leg bent, his knee like a prow cleaving the waves, behind him his left leg extended like a wing, or rather, like an oar (his leap calls to mind flying, which in turn calls to mind swimming) and his long tail tracing a spiral: a line/a liana/the Milky Way, his one arm upraised, encircled by heavy bracelets, and the huge hand clutching a warclub, his other arm thrust forward, with the fingers of the hand spread apart like a fan or the leaf of a royal palm or like the fin of a fish or the crest of a bird (again: swimming and flying), his skull enclosed in a helmet—a fiery red meteor hurtling through space.

Like his father Vāyu, the Great Monkey "traces signs of fire in the sky if he flies; if he falls, he leaves a tail of sounds on the earth: we hear his roar but do not see his form." Hanumān, like his father, is wind, and that is why his leaps are like the flight of birds; and while he is air, he is also sound with meaning: an emitter of words, a poet. Son of the wind, poet and grammarian, Hanumān is the divine messenger, the Holy Spirit of India. He is a monkey that is a bird that is a vital and spiritual breath. Though he is chaste, his body is an inexhaustible fountain of sperm, and a single drop of sweat from his skin suffices to make the stone womb of a desert fecund. Hanumān is the friend, the counselor, and the inspirer of the poet Vālmīki. Since legend has it that the author of the *Rāmāyana* was a pariah suffering from leprosy, the pariahs of Galta, who particularly venerate Hanumān, have taken the name of the poet for their own and hence are called Balmiks. But on that altar, a black stone daubed with thick red pigment, bathed in the liquid butter of the oblations, Hanumān was above all the Fire of the sacrifice. A priest had lighted a little brazier that

146

one of his acolytes had brought to him. Although naked from the waist up, he was not a Brahman and was not wearing the ritual cord around his neck; like the other officiants and like the majority of those present, he was a pariah. Turning his back to the worshipers who had crowded into the little sanctuary, he raised the brazier to the level of his eyes, and swinging it slowly up and down and in the direction of the eight points of the compass, he traced luminous circles and spirals in the air. The coals sizzled and smoked, the priest chanted the prayers in a whining nasal voice, and the other officiants, in accordance with the prescribed ritual, one by one cast spoonsful of melted butter into the fire: *The streams of butter gush forth (the golden rod in the center), they flow like rivers, they separate and flee like gazelles before the hunter, they leap about like women going to a love-tryst, the spoonsful of butter caress the burned wood, and the Fire accepts them with pleasure.*

With stones, little hammers, and other objects, the acolytes began to strike the iron bars hanging from the ceiling. A man appeared—wearing a coarse-woven garment, with a mask over his face, a helmet, and a rod simulating a lance. He may have represented one of the warrior monkeys who accompanied Hanumān and Sugriva on their expedition to Lankā. The acolytes continued to strike the iron bars, and a powerful and implacable storm of sound rained down on the heads of the

147

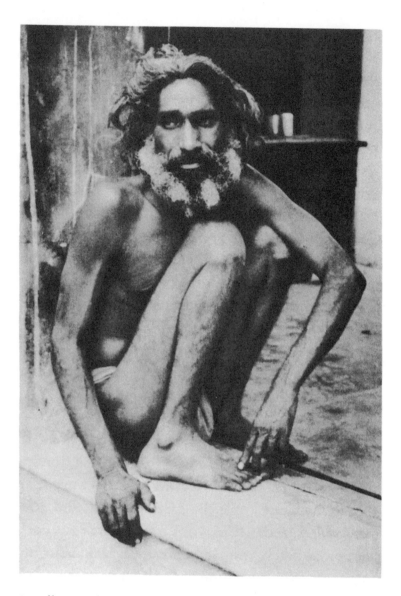

A sādhu in the sanctuary of Galta (photograph by Eusebio Rojas).

A sādhu and pilgrim near Galta (photograph by Eusebio Rojas).

multitude eddying about below. At the foot of the banyan tree a dozen *sādhus* had congregated, all of them advanced in years, with shaved heads or long tangled locks coated with red dust, wavy white beards, their faces smeared with paint and their foreheads decorated with signs: vertical and horizontal stripes, circles, half-moons, tridents. Some of them were decked in white or saffron robes, others were naked, their bodies covered with ashes or cow dung, their genitals protected by a cotton pouch hanging from a cord that served as a belt. Lying stretched out on the ground, they were smoking, drinking tea or milk or bhang, laughing, conversing, praying in a half-whisper, or simply lying there silently. On hearing the sound of the bars being struck and the confused murmur of the priests' voices chanting hymns overhead, they all stood up and without forewarning, as though obeying an order that no one save them had heard, with blazing eyes and somnambulistic gestures— the gestures of someone walking in his sleep and moving about very slowly, like a diver at the bottom of the sea— they formed a circle and began to sing and dance. The crowd gathered round and followed their movements, transfixed, with smiling, respectful fascination. Leaps and chants, the flutter of bright-colored rags and sparkling tatters, luxurious poverty, flashes of splendor and wretchedness, a dance of invalids and nonagenarians, the gestures of drowned men and illuminati, dry branches of the human tree that the wind rips off and carries away, a flight of puppets, the rasping voices of stones falling in blind wells, the piercing voices of panes of glass shattering, acts of homage paid by death to life.

The multitude was a lake of quiet movements, one vast warm undulation. The springs had let go, the tensions were disappearing, to exist was to spread out, to overflow, to turn liquid, to return to the primordial water, to the ocean that is the mother of all. The dance of the *sādhus*, the chants of the officiants, the cries and exclamations of the multitude were bubbles rising from the great lake lying hypnotized beneath the metallic rain brought forth by the acolytes as they struck the iron bars. In the sky overhead, insensible to the movements of the hordes of people jammed together in the courtyard and to their rites, the crows, the blackbirds, the vultures, and the parakeets imperturbably continued their flights, their disputes, and their lovemaking. A limpid, naked sky. The air too had ceased to move. Calm and indifference. A deceptive repose made up of thousands upon thousands of imperceptible changes and movements: although it appeared that the light had halted forever on the pink scar on the wall, the stone was throbbing, breathing, it was alive, its scar was becoming more and more inflamed until finally it turned into a great gaping red wound, and just as this smoldering coal was about to burst into flame, it changed its

151

mind, contracted little by little, withdrew into itself, buried itself in its dying ardor, simply a black stain spreading over the wall now. It was the same with the sky, with the courtyard, with the crowd. Evening came amid the fallen brightnesses, submerged the flat-topped hills, blinded the reflections, turned the transparencies opaque. Congregating on the balconies from which, in other times, the princes and their wives contemplated the spectacles taking place on the esplanade, hundreds and hundreds of monkeys, with that curiosity of theirs that is a terrible form of the indifference of the universe, watched the feast being celebrated by the men down below.

 When spoken or written, words advance and inscribe themselves one after the other upon the space that is theirs: the sheet of paper, the wall of air. They advance, they go from here to there, they trace a path: they go by, they are time. Although they never stop moving from one point to another and thus describe a horizontal or vertical line (depending on the nature of the writing), from another perspective, the simultaneous or converging one which is that of poetry, the phrases that go to make up a text appear as great motionless, transparent blocks: the text does not go anywhere, language ceases to flow. A dizzying repose because it is a fabric woven of nothing but clarity: each page reflects all the others, and each one is the echo of the one that precedes or follows it—the echo and the answer, rhyme and metaphor. There is no end and no beginning: everything is center. Neither before nor after, neither in front of nor behind, neither inside nor outside: everything is in everything. Like a spiral sea-

Bharat transporting Hanumān to battlefield with his magic arrow, Oudh, 19th century.

shell, all times are this time now, which is nothing except, like cut crystal, the momentary condensation of other times into an insubstantial clarity. Condensation and dispersion, the secret sign that the now makes to itself just as it dissipates. Simultaneous perspective does not look upon language as a path because it is not the search for meaning that orients it. Poetry does not attempt to discover what there is at the end of the road; it conceives of the text as a series of transparent strata within which the various parts—the different verbal and semantic currents—produce momentary configurations as they intertwine or break apart, as they reflect each other or efface each other. Poetry contemplates itself, fuses with itself, and obliterates itself in the crystallizations of language. Apparitions, metamorphoses, volatilizations, precipitations of presences. These configurations are crystallized time: although they are perpetually in motion, they always point to the same hour—the hour of change. Each one of them contains all the others, each one is inside the others: change is only the oft-repeated and ever-different metaphor of identity.

The vision of poetry is that of the convergence of every point. The end of the road. This is the vision of Hanumān as he leaps (a geyser) from the valley to the mountaintop or as he plunges (a meteorite) from the star to the bottom of the sea: the dizzying oblique vision that reveals the universe not as a succession, a movement, but as an assemblage of spaces and times, a repose. Convergence is repose because at its apex the various movements, as they meet, obliterate each other; at the same time, from this peak of immobility, we perceive the universe as an assemblage of worlds in rotation. Poems: crystallizations of the universal play of analogy, transparent objects which, as they reproduce the mechanism and the rotary motion of analogy, are waterspouts of new analogies. In them the world plays at being the world, which is the game of similarities engendered by differences and that of contradictory similarities. Hanumān wrote on the rocky cliffs of a mountain the *Mahanātaka*, based on the same subject as the *Rāmāyana*; on reading it, Vālmīki feared that it would overshadow his poem and begged Hanumān to keep his drama a secret. The Monkey yielded to the poet's entreaty, uprooted the mountain, and threw the rocks into the sea. Vālmīki's pen and ink on the paper are a metaphor of the bolt of lightning and the rain with which Hanumān wrote his drama on the rocky mountainside. Human writing reflects that of the universe, it is its translation, but also its metaphor: it says something totally different and it says the same thing. At the point of convergence the play of similarities and differences cancels itself out in order that identity alone may shine forth. The illusion of motionlessness, the play of mirrors of the one: identity is completely empty; it is a crystallization and in its transparent core the movement of analogy begins all over once again.

All poems say the same thing and each poem is unique. Each part reproduces the others and each part is different. As I began these pages I decided to follow literally the metaphor of the title of the collection that they were intended for, the Paths of Creation, and to write, to describe a text that was really a path and that could be read and followed as such. As I wrote, the path to Galta grew blurred or else I lost my bearings and went astray in the trackless wilds. Again and again I was obliged to return to the starting point. Instead of advancing, the text circled about itself. Is destruction creation? I do not know, but I do know that creation is not destruction. At each turn the text opened out into another one, at once its translation and its transposition: a spiral of repetitions and reiterations that have dissolved into a negation of writing as a path. Today I realize that my text was not going anywhere—except to meet itself. I also perceive that repetitions are metaphors and that reiterations are analogies: a system of mirrors that little by little have revealed another text. In this text Hanumān contemplates the garden of Rāvana like a page of calligraphy like the harem of the same Rāvana as described in the *Rāmāyana* like this page on which the swaying motions of the beeches in the grove opposite

157

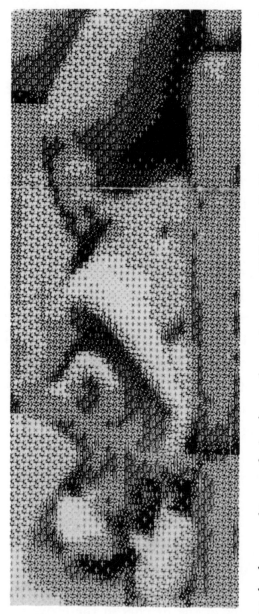

Nude, photographic proof taken by an electronic process, 1968, Leon D. Harmon (artist) and Kenneth C. Knowlton (engineer), (University of California).

my window accumulate on this page like the shadows of two lovers projected by the fire on a wall like the stains of monsoon rains on a ruined palace of the abandoned town of Galta like the rectangular space on which there surge the wave upon wave of a multitude contemplated from the crumbling balconies by hundreds of monkeys like an image of writing and reading like a metaphor of the path and the pilgrimage to the sanctuary like the final dissolution of the path and the convergence of all the texts in this paragraph like a metaphor of the embrace of bodies. Analogy: universal transparency: seeing in this that.

29

The body of Splendor as it divides, dis-
perses, dissipates itself in my body as it
divides, disperses, dissipates itself in the
body of Splendor:

breathing, warmth, outline, bulk that
beneath the pressure of my fingertips
slowly ceases to be a confusion of pulses and gathers itself
together and reunites with itself,

vibrations, waves that strike my closed eyelids as the
street lamps go out and dawn staggers through the city:

the body of Splendor before my eyes that gaze down
on her as she lies between the sheets as I walk toward her
in the dawn in the green light filtering through the
enormous leaves of a banana tree onto an ocher footpath
to Galta that leads me to this page where the body of
Splendor lies between the sheets as I write on this page
and as I read what I write,

an ocher footpath that suddenly starts walking, a
river of burned waters seeking its path between the
sheets, Splendor rises from the bed and walks about in

The palace of Galta (18th century), (photograph by Eusebio Rojas).

the shadowy light of the room with staggering steps as the street lamps of the city go out:

she is searching for something, the dawn is searching for something, the young woman halts and looks at me: a squirrel gaze, a dawn gaze that lingers amid the leaves of the banyan tree along the ocher path that leads from Galta to this page, a gaze that is a well to be drunk from, a gaze in which I write the word reconciliation:

Splendor is this page, that which separates (liberates) and weaves together (reconciles) the various parts that compose it,

that which (the one who) is there, at the end of what I say, at the end of this page, and appears here as this phrase is uttered, as it dissipates,

the act inscribed on this page and the bodies (the phrases) that as they embrace give form to this act, this body:

the liturgical sequence and the dissipation of all rites through the double profanation (yours and mine), the reconciliation/liberation, of writing and reading

Cambridge, England, summer, 1970

162